HOW I SURVIVED MIDDLE SCHOOL

P.S. I Really Like You

By Nancy Krulik

SCHOLASTIC INC.

New York   Toronto   London   Auckland   Sydney
Mexico City   New Delhi   Hong Kong   Buenos Aires

ISBN-13: 978-0-545-01942-2
ISBN-10: 0-545-01942-7

Published by Scholastic Inc. SCHOLASTIC and associated logos are trademarks and/or registered trademarks of Scholastic Inc.

12 11 10 9 8 7   9 10 11 12 13/0

Printed in the U.S.A.
First printing, January 2008
Book design by Alison Klapthor

For Marie and Sheila, who are helping me survive the middle school experience.
P.S. I really like you!

Check out these other books in the
How I Survived Middle School series by Nancy Krulik:

Can You Get an F in Lunch?

Madame President

I Heard a Rumor

The New Girl

Cheat Sheet

Are You Crushin' on Him?

Is there one special guy you think about all the time? Are you happy just being pals, or do you want more? In other words, do you just like him, or do you *like* him, like him? There's only one way to find out how badly you're crushin' on your guy. You've gotta take this quiz!

1. When you first saw your crush, how did you feel about him?

A. I thought he was the cutest guy I'd ever seen and I wanted to meet him right away!

B. I thought he was cute, but so was the guy sitting two rows behind him.

C. He looked kind of nice and I wanted to get to know him.

2. How would you react if you heard your crush was moving away?

A. I'd make sure we had each others' e-mail addies so we could keep in touch.

B. I can't even think about that — it hurts too much.

C. I'd start looking around for my next crush. Life goes on, you know?

3. **You and your crush are in the same math class. How does this affect you?**

A. Even though I'd like to look over at him constantly, I force myself to stay focused on my work. I want to make honor roll this marking period.

B. I spend the whole class staring at him, and making sure no one is passing him notes except me.

C. Every now and then I catch myself looking at him instead of doing my work.

4. **Right before you go to sleep, you . . .**

A. Think about your crush so you're sure to dream about him.

B. Check your e-mail to see if your crush sent you a message.

C. Get your outfit and book bag ready for the next day.

5. **It's a rainy, yucky Saturday. How do you spend the afternoon?**

A. Baking a batch of yummy cookies

B. Dialing his number over and over again, just so you can hear his voice when he picks up

C. Making plans to go to the movies with a bunch of friends. You call and *personally* invite your crush, of course.

6. When you're watching TV, you . . .

A. Mentally compare every guy on the screen to Mr. Crush. Sometimes he's cuter, sometimes they are.

B. Turn down the sound and grab the phone if it rings — it could be one of your friends calling with some good gossip (about your crush, hopefully!).

C. Do your homework — even though you're not supposed to do it with the TV on.

7. You've got an appointment for a haircut. How do you prep for it?

A. You pore through magazines, searching for one that will make you look like a movie star so he'll definitely notice you.

B. You don't. It's just a trim.

C. Have your BFF ask your crush if he likes girls better with short hair or long — and then go with whatever he tells her.

8. Someone tells you that your crush is absent today. How do you feel?

A. Bummed. Without him to stare at, English class will be a total bore.

B. Really worried. In fact, you call him three times during the day to see if he's feeling better.

C. Relieved that there won't be any distractions while you take your French test later in the day.

Now total up your points, and check the chart to see just how deep your crush goes.

1. A. 3 points   B. 2 points   C. 1 point
2. A. 2 points   B. 3 points   C. 1 point
3. A. 1 point   B. 3 points   C. 2 points
4. A. 3 points   B. 2 points   C. 1 point
5. A. 1 point   B. 3 points   C. 2 points
6. A. 3 points   B. 2 points   C. 1 point
7. A. 2 points   B. 1 point   C. 3 points
8. A. 2 points   B. 3 points   C. 1 point

8–14 points: You're not really crushing. It's more likely that you've found yourself a good pal who just happens to be a guy. But that's okay. You can never have too many pals. And remember, boyfriends come and go, but boys who are friends stick around.

15–20 points: It's official: You are definitely crushing on him! However, you're managing to go about your biz and also concentrating on things besides the object of your affection. You know the secret to a healthy crush — it's all about balancing him and the rest of your life.

21–24 points: Uh-oh! This crush is crushing you! You can't think about anything but your guy, and that's not good. It's time for you to channel all that energy into something else. How about signing up for a soccer clinic or a photography club? You just might discover a talent you never knew you had!

Chapter
ONE

I, JENNY McAFEE, hate first period English class.

And I have a really good reason. English is the toughest class I have all day, and it comes first thing in the morning. How rotten is that?

Don't get me wrong. I don't hate *everything* about English. I love to read, and I write poetry and stories on my own. But Ms. Jaffe, our English teacher, is the toughest, strictest teacher in all of Joyce Kilmer Middle School. She's mega-serious about stuff like making sure you have the correct heading on your paper and using proper grammar all the time. And you wouldn't believe how tough she is when it comes to grading papers!

Worst of all, Ms. Jaffe usually makes us read our work out loud, so the rest of the class can critique it. I *really* can't stand that. Speaking in public is one of my least favorite things to do in the world. I read a poll once that said speaking in public is the thing people fear the most — even more than being kidnapped or dying! That sounds pretty weird, I know. But I understand it. Speaking to a room full of people who are all staring right at you is pretty scary. At least it is to me.

Addie Wilson, on the other hand, has no fear of public speaking. In fact, she's really comfortable with being the center of attention. That's why she was the first person to raise her hand this morning when Ms. Jaffe asked for a volunteer to read their persuasive essay. Ms. Jaffe really liked that Addie volunteered. And I'm sure that Addie, who really likes being liked, had planned on that.

"My essay is called *Keep the World Green*," Addie said as she stood up and walked to the front of the room. "Joyce Kilmer Middle School needs an environmental club so that the school can become more ecologically friendly," she began.

I leaned back in my chair and tried to focus on what Addie was saying. But I was more fascinated by what she was wearing. Her long black shirt hung loosely over her black and silver leggings. And her silver hoop earrings and sparkly silver ballet slippers pulled the outfit together perfectly.

I put my hand to my hole-less earlobes and sighed. My mother won't let me get my ears pierced until I'm thirteen. I'm only eleven. Two years — that's like an eternity! Not that earrings would make any difference. If I tried putting an outfit like Addie's together, I would've looked like a mutant ballerina. But Addie has a flair for throwing things like that together so they just work. She's always been like that — ever since we were kids. I remember playing dress-up with her in her mother's closet when we were younger. I always wound up looking ridiculous — clomping around in high heels with some huge straw hat on my head and lipstick on my teeth. Addie would wear her mother's skirt as a strapless dress, throw a scarf around her neck, wrap a few strands of beads around her wrists, and come out looking like a mini-model.

Of course, that was back when we were in elementary school and Addie and I were BFF. It wasn't how things were today. We'd only been in middle school for a few months, but elementary school may as well have been ancient history considering how different things were between Addie and me now. Sometime during the summer between fifth grade graduation and the first day of middle school, while I was at sleepaway camp, Addie had decided that she was much cooler than I was and that we weren't friends anymore. That was it. I hadn't had any say in the matter at all.

Not that I would have liked to hang out with Addie's new group of friends. I definitely would not have fit in with the Pops. That's what my friends and I call Addie and her friends. The Pops. As in *Pop*ular.

Nearly everyone in our school wants to be one of the Pops — even if they won't admit it out loud. Their secret longing shows up in the way lots of the non-Pops try to dress like them, talk like them, and laugh at the jokes Addie and her friends make in the hall.

But no matter how hard the wannabee Pops might try, *everyone* can't be a Pop. It's a very exclusive group.

I have a lot of friends. It's not like I sit alone at lunch or have nothing to do after school or on the weekends. But in our school having a lot of friends isn't what makes you popular. To be popular, people have to want to be in your group. And no one's dying to be one of us. But that's okay. My friends like one another, we're here for one another, and we have a great time together. What more do you need?

"Lots of movie stars are driving cars that run on a combination of gasoline and electricity," Addie continued, reading from her paper. "These cars are called hybrids and they're better for our environment because they use less gas. We should all do the same thing. Now is the time to go green!"

I sat there quietly in my seat, staring into space while Addie's voice droned on and on in my ears. I was using a skill that is very important in middle school — even though it's not something you'll find in the handbook they give you at the sixth grade orientation.

MIDDLE SCHOOL RULE # 23:

LEARN TO SLEEP WITH YOUR EYES OPEN AND YOUR BACK STRAIGHT. TEACHERS ONLY GET MAD WHEN YOU PUT YOUR HEAD ON THE DESK.

"And that is why I think Joyce Kilmer Middle School needs an environmental club," Addie finished up. "We need to do our part to save the planet."

"That was terrific, Addie," Ms. Jaffe congratulated her. She looked around the classroom, glancing fleetingly at each of us, until her eyes finally landed on her next victim — me. "Jenny, what are your thoughts on Addie's essay? Was she persuasive?"

I jumped at the sound of my name. There are no other Jennys in our class, so she was definitely talking to me. Which meant I had to say something, and fast. Ms. Jaffe wouldn't be happy if she knew I'd drifted off.

"Um . . . yeah . . . she was persuasive," I said. *Not a very persuasive answer on my part, huh?*

"Why don't you elaborate on that?" Ms. Jaffe suggested.

"Well, I think the part about the movie stars was kind of interesting," I said, repeating the only part of Addie's speech I could recall.

Ms. Jaffe nodded. "Public figures can sometimes be good role models," she agreed.

Addie smiled proudly. And I knew why. At our school, Addie was sort of like a movie star. She wasn't an actress or anything, but she and the other Pops were our school celebrities. Which meant that, like the actors in Hollywood, all eyes were on them all the time.

"Addie, I think your idea of an environmental club is a good one," Ms. Jaffe said. "In fact, I think that the entire sixth grade should make preserving the environment their top priority. It can be the sixth grade class project."

The *what?* I'd never heard of a sixth grade class project before. It wasn't in the middle school orientation handbook.

"Every year, each grade takes on a community service project," Ms. Jaffe explained, as though she were reading my mind. "Last year, the sixth graders collected soap, shampoo, toothpaste, and toothbrushes for people who live in homeless shelters. This year I think an environmental project would be fantastic! And since this was your idea, Addie, you should be in charge."

That was all it took. Addie was smiling so broadly now I thought her teeth were going to fall out of her mouth. There was nothing Addie Wilson liked more than being in charge.

"Oh, man," my friend Chloe groaned under her breath.

I knew exactly what Chloe meant. Take one part Addie Wilson, stir in a little power, and you have a recipe for disaster.

But there was nothing we could do about it. Ms. Jaffe had made up her mind, and that was that. Addie was in charge of the sixth grade environment class project and we were all going to have to follow her lead.

"I wonder what putting all of that hot air into the atmosphere does to the environment?" Chloe joked as she and I plopped down at our lunch table later that day. We were in the process of telling our group of friends all about what had happened in English class that morning.

That's what I love most about Chloe. She has the guts to say out loud the things that other people only dare to think.

"That was a pretty long speech," I agreed with a giggle.

"And leave it to Addie to be all into the environment because movie stars are talking about it," Chloe continued.

"Addie is definitely a poser," our friend Sam agreed. "She thinks she's so rad."

"So what?" Chloe asked.

"Rad," Sam repeated in her British accent. "You know, cool."

I shook my head. "Addie *is* cool," I corrected my friend. "At least by our school's standards."

Sam shrugged. It was obvious that she didn't agree. Not that I was surprised. Sam has a different cool-measuring barometer than the rest of us. I think it's because she moved here from England not too long ago, and she's pretty cool herself. She's always wearing amazing European clothes and she even has a funky hot pink streak in her hair.

"If you say so," Sam said, obviously not wanting to get into another what's-so-special-about-the-Pops discussion. "Anyway, the thing is, Addie's right about this school not being eco-friendly. We waste so much. Look at the way we fill all the rubbish bins with perfectly good scrap paper."

"And how about these Styrofoam cups they serve the punch in?" our pal Josh added, lifting a white cup from his tray. "It will take 50 years for it to biodegrade. And it will be *450* years before those plastic water bottles decompose!" he added, pointing to the water bottles that our friends Marilyn and Carolyn had on their trays.

The twins looked sheepishly at each other. Then they both shrugged, picked up their bottles, and simultaneously took sips of water. I had to laugh. Synchronized sipping. A new Olympic sport.

"Whoa! Another science lesson from Mr. Wizard," our friend Marc teased Josh. "Dude, you are amazing!" he added sincerely.

I knew exactly what Marc meant. We all knew Josh was smart. But the way he could just pull facts like that right out of the air was pretty astounding.

"I get the whole save-the-environment thing," Chloe agreed, "but you're missing the point, Josh."

"What *is* the point?" he wondered.

"The point is, Addie's in charge. That means we all have to do what she says," Chloe reminded him. "Do you know how awful that's gonna be?"

"Maybe it won't be *too* horrible," our friend Liza suggested reasonably. "You guys will all be working together, and that could be kinda fun. And besides, no matter how horrible Addie acts, at least you know that you're doing something very important."

"That's easy for you to say," Chloe told Liza. "You're in *seventh* grade. You don't have to be involved with this."

I had to agree with Chloe on that one. As seventh graders, Liza, the twins, and Marc wouldn't be working on this project. Addie wouldn't be able to boss any of them around.

"All Addie has ever wanted is to be in charge of something," Liza insisted. "And she's been really bummed ever since Jenny beat her out for class president."

That was true. Addie had been kind of mad about losing the election to me. She had been sure she would win. Everyone had been sure of it — even me.

"Maybe that's why she's been so mean," Liza continued. "Now that she's got something to take charge of, she'll probably be nicer to people."

"It's possible," I agreed slowly, hoping Liza was right.

Still, as I watched Addie and her Pop pals make their way across the cafeteria to the girls room — their special lunchtime clubhouse — I couldn't help noticing they were all still pointing at people and whispering and giggling. Addie hadn't changed. At least not yet.

Chapter
TWO

ADDIE DIDN'T WASTE ANY TIME making sure the whole sixth grade knew who was in charge of our class environment project. By the next morning, she had an entire plan ready to show Ms. Jaffe. And the day after that, the whole sixth grade was herded together into the auditorium for a special assembly during last period.

As we filed into our seats, I looked up at the stage. There were three people sitting there – Ms. Jaffe, our principal, Ms. Gold, and of course, Addie. Dana Harrison (the only other sixth grade Pop girl) and her friend, Aaron, were right in the front row, cheering Addie on. My friends and I slipped into our usual spots – somewhere toward the middle of the auditorium near the side.

"You guys want to come hang out at my house after school?" I asked them. "I barely have any homework tonight."

"Me, neither," Chloe agreed. "Sure, I guess. I have to call home first, though."

Sam nodded. "I'll ring my mum and make sure she's cool with it."

"How about you guys?" I asked, looking down the row to where our friends Felicia and Rachel were sitting.

Rachel shook her head. "Count us out for the next week," she said. "Basketball practice."

"For the CHAMPIONSHIP!" Felicia added, pumping her hands in the air.

"Oh, did our school team make the championship?" I teased her.

We all laughed at that. The championship was all Felicia and Rachel had been talking about. Not that I blamed them. It was a huge deal. The whole school was talking about how our girls' basketball team had made the league championship. My friends and I were especially psyched about it because Felicia and Rachel were the only sixth graders on the team.

"You guys are coming, aren't you?" Felicia asked. "I mean, I know Josh will be there, because he promised. . . ."

"And because he wants to see you in shorts," Sam teased her.

Felicia blushed. But I could tell she was pleased. She loved it when people brought up the fact that Josh was her boyfriend — almost as much as Josh was embarrassed by it. I was really glad he hadn't gotten to the auditorium yet. That comment would have totally mortified him.

"We'll all be there," I assured Felicia.

But for now we were all *here*, in the auditorium, waiting for Addie to take center stage. Which she happily did after an introduction by Ms. Gold.

"I think our first project should be setting up a

recycling system for our school," Addie told everyone. "My plan is for us to purchase special trash cans for recyclable paper, plastics, and metal. We'll have a big campaign to get everyone interested in separating their trash."

I found myself nodding in agreement with Addie, despite myself. It was hard to argue with her. The plan made sense. Recycling *was* good for the environment.

"Of course, that will all take money," Addie continued. "Which we'll have to raise ourselves."

"I'll bet she has a plan for that, too," Chloe whispered in my ear.

"But don't worry, I have a plan for that, too," Addie said from the stage.

Chloe and I burst out laughing, but we stopped when we got a stern glance from Señorita Gonzalez, our Spanish teacher.

"We're going to have a candy fund-raiser," Addie continued. "But not a boring old sell-chocolate-bars kind of fund-raiser. What I'm planning is *much* more exciting. Everyone in the school will have a chance to show their friends how much they adore them by buying them bags of jelly beans. The sixth grade will have a table set up at the championship basketball game, and for a few days afterward. We want to give everyone a chance to be a part of this."

"Oh, joy," Chloe moaned, sinking into her chair and yawning with boredom. I had to fight the urge to laugh.

"When you order a bag of candy, you'll be able to fill out a notecard on recycled paper so your friend knows who it's from. Then, members of the student council will go from classroom to classroom delivering the candy. I've already discussed this with Sandee Wind. As head of the student council she assured me that all of the representatives will help us in any way they can."

"I can't believe it! She went right over your head to Sandee," Rachel whispered to me. "I thought she was supposed to run any student council ideas by you before she talked to Sandee about them. After all *you're* the sixth grade class president. She's only the *vice* president."

I sighed. Rachel was right. Addie had found a way to take charge of everything without including me. But I couldn't get all freaked out about it. After all, there was something much more upsetting about Addie's plan.

"Leave it to Addie to turn an environmental project into a popularity contest," I groaned as I stood at my locker with Chloe, Liza, and Sam at the end of the day.

"Huh?" Sam asked me. "What contest? All I heard was that we were ordering candy for our friends."

"Which will be delivered during the day — in front of everyone," I reminded her.

"And the Pops will get more candy than anyone else," Chloe added, suddenly catching on.

"Exactly," I said.

"Oh," Sam chimed in as it all became clear. "That was quite clever of her."

"This is just another way for Addie to show people how popular she is," Chloe groaned. "I can't believe I missed that."

I couldn't believe it, either. Usually Chloe was the first to catch on to a Pop trick. But she'd missed this one completely. I was surprised no one else had picked up on it either — especially not the teachers like Ms. Jaffe. But I guess that's what's so amazing about Pop-magic. The Pops give the illusion of being really nice, and everybody — especially grown-ups — falls for it.

"Of course, you know this could backfire," Chloe said after a moment. "The Pops aren't nearly as beloved as they think they are."

"I think they're actually kind of feared more than anything else," Liza pointed out. "People don't buy candy for people they're afraid of. I bet the only people buying jelly beans for the Pops will be other Pops."

"And since there's a limited number of Pops, there's a limited amount of candy they'll get," Chloe added. "We might even get more than they do."

"Unless the Pops have a bunch of secret admirers out there we don't know about," I suggested.

Chloe giggled. "I doubt it. The Pops are their own biggest admirers. And they don't ever make a secret of it."

I looked over my shoulder toward Addie's locker where the girl Pops — Addie, Dana, Claire, Maya, and

Sabrina — were gathered together. Dana was staring at us with an angry glint in her eye. She looked kind of annoyed that we were in the same hallway as her.

She would have been a whole lot more annoyed if she'd heard what my friends and I had just been saying. Luckily, we'd been talking pretty quietly. At least I hoped we had been.

"Do you guys want to eat dinner over here?" I asked Sam and Chloe that evening. We'd been hanging out together at my house all afternoon, giving one another manicures, playing with my pet mice, and doing quizzes on my favorite website, middleschoolsurvival.com. I'd found the site one afternoon at the beginning of the school year, when I was miserable and friendless after Addie had dumped me for the Pops. Taking some of those quizzes had helped me figure out that Addie and I were never going to be BFF again, and that my new friends were a much better match for me. The site also has delicious recipes and even tips on school stuff like taking notes and studying successfully. It totally rocks!

Chloe sniffed at the air. "Something does smell delicious," she noted.

"That's my dad's chili," I told her. "It's super spicy. He says it's the best chili north of Mexico."

"Sounds good to me," Chloe said, pulling out her cell.

"Me, too," Sam said. "I love spicy food."

As soon as Chloe and Sam had permission from their moms to stay for dinner, we all trekked downstairs to the kitchen. Sure enough, my dad was there, wearing his "Kiss the Cook" apron, and boiling something on the stove.

"Better add some more hamburger meat, Dad," I told him. "Both Chloe's and Sam's moms said they could have dinner here."

"Excellent!" my father exclaimed. "You girls are going to love my chili. It's the best chili . . ."

"North of Mexico," Sam, Chloe, and I said in unison.

Dad looked pretty pleased. "So you've heard of it?" he asked proudly.

Chloe gave me a wink. "Oh, yeah. You're very famous."

Dad grinned.

"Is there anything we can do to help?" Sam asked him. "Maybe we can cut up the onions or something?"

"Oh, no," my dad told her. "This is a secret recipe. I'm the only one who works on my chili." He stopped and looked at Sam's disappointed face. "But you can make something else if you'd like. Maybe dessert or a side dish." He turned to me. "Do you still have that recipe for the chocolate chip bars you made the other day?"

I knew exactly what recipe he meant. They were these unbelievably scrumptious snacks I'd baked last Saturday afternoon while it was raining. I'd found the recipe on middleschoolsurvival.com. "I've got it bookmarked upstairs," I said, rushing toward the stairs. "I'll go print it out. I'll be right back."

A few minutes later, I was back in the kitchen with the recipe. My friends and I read it carefully and then began gathering the materials.

Chocolate Chip Buttery Bites

You will need:

    2 cups all-purpose flour
    1/2 tsp. baking soda
    1 cup brown sugar
    1 cup butter, softened
    1 egg
    2 tsp. vanilla extract
    1 1/2 cups semi-sweet chocolate chips
    1 cup chopped pecans

Here's what you do:

1. First, ask an adult for help. Then preheat the oven to 300 degrees F.
2. Grease an 8 x 8-inch baking pan.
3. Combine flour and baking soda in a medium bowl and set aside.
4. Use an electric mixer to blend the sugar and butter. Then add the egg and vanilla and beat at medium speed until smooth.
5. Add flour mixture and blend on low speed until combined. Be careful not to over-mix. Stir in chocolate chips and pecans.
6. Pour the batter into the greased baking pan.
7. Bake in the center of the oven for 35-45 minutes. (To test if it's done, stick a toothpick into the center of the pan. If the toothpick comes out clean, it's done.)
8. Cool on a rack.
9. Ask an adult to use a sharp knife to cut 1 x 2-inch bars. Makes 16 snacks.

"This seems pretty easy," Chloe said.

"Just don't ask me to crack the egg," Sam said. "I'm kind of cack-handed."

"Kind of what?" Chloe asked her.

"Clumsy," Sam explained. "I always wind up getting eggshell into the batter when my mum and I bake."

"Do you bake a lot?" I asked.

Sam nodded. "One day you guys will have to taste my Yorkshire pudding."

"Why would you bake *pudding*?" Chloe asked her.

"It's not pudding like American chocolate pudding," Sam told her. "Yorkshire pudding is more like a popover. It's made with flour, salt, milk, and eggs. You bake it in the oven. It's really good with roast beef."

"Sounds amazing," I told her.

"It's brill," Sam assured me. "Totally." Then she smiled. "I just love being in the kitchen. It's always so warm and cozy."

My dad chose that exact moment to suddenly break into song. *"Someone's in the kitchen with Dinah, some- one's in the kitchen I know-oh-oh . . ."*

I stood there for a minute, feeling the blood rush into my cheeks. My dad sings in the kitchen all the time. In fact, I never really notice it — until someone else is over. And then it's kinda embarrassing. So I stood there for a minute, waiting for Chloe or Sam to laugh, or make some crack about my totally nerdy dad.

But instead, Chloe started singing along with him. *"Someone's in the kitchen with Dinah, strummin' on the old banjo."*

"What are you guys singing?" Sam asked them.

My father stopped stirring the chili and stared at her. "You've never heard 'I've Been Working on the Railroad'?" he asked her.

Sam shook her head.

"It's an *American* folk song, Dad," I reminded him.

Dad grinned at Sam. "Well, if you're gonna live here, this is one you've gotta know!" And he began to sing the whole song, from the top. *"I've been working on the railroad. . . ."*

"All the live-long day," Chloe chimed in.

A few minutes later, we were all singing *"Fee-fi-fiddlee-i-oh"* in the kitchen with my dad. As I looked around, I knew for sure that my new friends were the best friends anyone could ever have. And it didn't matter if none of them gave me any jelly beans. I was just lucky to have them to hang around with.

"Someone's in the kitchen with Dinah," I sang out even louder. *"Strummin' on the old banjo. . . ."*

Chapter
THREE

"SO THEN, MAYA CALLED ME and told me this great idea she had for . . ." Addie *had* been talking to Dana. But she stopped the conversation the second I walked past her desk in English class the next morning. Obviously, whatever she was saying, she didn't want me to hear.

Like I'd want to hear anything she had to say, anyway.

Well, I would, actually. And I'm not completely sure why. I mean, it probably wasn't anything important or interesting, but I still wanted to know what it was. Maybe it was the fact that Addie used to tell me everything, or maybe it was just my curiosity about what it was like to be a Pop and talk about Pop stuff, but I wanted to know.

I sighed heavily and dropped my books on my desk. Then I went over to talk to Sam for a while. Not that I had anything particular to talk about, but hey, Addie and Dana weren't the only ones who could have a private conversation. I purposely turned my back to them and spoke really low, so they would think I was saying something private, too, even though I wasn't.

"Hey," I greeted Sam.

"I had gobs of fun at your house yesterday," she replied. "Your dad's a scream."

"He's pretty funny," I agreed.

"And those chocolate chip bars were truly scrumptious," she added. "We should bring some to the basketball game."

I nodded. "I always get hungry watching other people exercise," I said with a laugh.

Sam giggled, too. "I know what you mean," she agreed.

I glanced over my shoulder to see if Addie and Dana were wondering what Sam and I were laughing about. They weren't. They were too busy staring at some pictures on Dana's camera phone. Darn.

"Actually, I don't know how much of the game I'll get to see," I told Sam, sadly.

"What are you talking about?"

"I got an e-mail from Sandee Wind last night," I explained. "Apparently, student council members are the ones who will be taking orders for the jelly bean deliveries during the game."

"The whole game?" Sam asked, sounding a little sorry for me.

I shook my head. "We're taking shifts. The sixth grade representatives – that's Addie and me – are working at the table during the final quarter."

"You and *Addie*?" Sam asked. Now she sounded *really* sorry for me.

I nodded. I knew what she meant. I felt really sorry for me, too.

A few minutes later, I took my assigned seat — between Chloe and Dana — and waited for Ms. Jaffe to come in. Addie turned around in her chair and shot me one of her incredibly phony smiles. "So I hear you and I are selling jelly beans together," she said.

I sighed slightly and nodded.

"I'm ordering matching T-shirts for all the student council members who are selling the jelly beans," Addie continued. "They're going to say 'Buy Jelly Beans for Your Favorite Human Beans.' Isn't that cute?"

"I think it's awesome," Dana remarked.

I didn't think it was so awesome, or cute. But there was no sense in telling Addie that. She wouldn't have cared what I thought.

"And we're all going to wear them at the game on Saturday," Addie continued.

"That's one time you'll be wearing an outfit as cool as Addie's," Dana told me. Then she looked over at Chloe. "Of course, after Saturday, no one will be wearing the T-shirts anymore, so you can give it to her. She can add it to her collection."

The way Dana said the word "collection," I could tell she didn't really approve of Chloe's clothing choices. Chloe wears a lot of funny T-shirts to school. Today she was wearing a lavender-colored one that read, "I want it all, and I want it delivered!" It wasn't exactly the up-to-the-minute fashion that Addie, Dana, and the other Pops liked to wear, but it was totally Chloe. And I thought it was hilarious.

"No, thanks," Chloe told Dana. "I only wear T-shirts that are really clever and unusual."

I couldn't believe Chloe had just had the guts to say that to the most popular girls in our entire grade. Or then again, maybe I could. Like I said, Chloe will say out loud what the rest of us will only think.

Addie's face turned as red as a beet, and I actually thought I saw steam pouring out of her ears. (Okay, not really. But if she was a cartoon, that's what would've happened.) She opened her mouth to speak, but at that moment, Ms. Jaffe walked into the room and began to write something on the board. Class had begun, which meant Chloe had gotten the last word. Score one for our side!

"Do you have the worksheet for English class?" Chloe asked me as she sat down across from me in the cafeteria at lunch. "I want to get some of it done now so I don't have so much homework to do tonight."

"I think so," I said, opening my binder and turning to the English section. As I reached into the folder and pulled out the worksheet, a small piece of paper — folded over four times — fell out with it. It was a note I'd never seen before. One of my friends must have slipped it into my folder when I wasn't looking.

I handed Chloe the worksheet she had asked for, and opened the note under the table, for privacy.

```
Dear Jenny,
You're the cutest girl in the whole sixth
grade. You're really smart, too. In fact, I
think you should be the most popular girl in our
school because you are so amazing.
From,
Your Secret Admirer
P.S. I really like you!
```

I gasped slightly, and I could feel the blood rising to my cheeks. I was blushing. I'm, like, a champion blusher. It doesn't take a lot for me to get embarrassed and turn pink. So a note like that was enough to turn my cheeks really red!

"Jenny, are you okay?" Sam asked me from across the table.

I quickly folded the note and slipped it into my jeans pocket. "Um, yeah. I um . . . It's just really hot in here. Don't you think?"

Sam shrugged. "Not really."

"Speaking of hot, Rachel told me the girls' basketball team is totally on fire," I said, trying to change the subject. I definitely didn't want to talk to my friends about the note. At least not yet. It was too weird.

"Yeah, it's going to be a good game," Josh agreed.

"Lincoln's a really strong team on defense, but our offense is much more aggressive."

We all stared at him. None of us had ever heard Josh discuss sports before, except tae kwon do, of course. Josh was a black belt.

"Boy, Felicia's really rubbing off on you," Marc said.

Now it was Josh's turn to blush. But he didn't deny it.

"Maybe we should use you as our commentator for our broadcast of the big game," Marc told him.

"What broadcast?" Liza asked.

"The film club's using digital video cameras to put the game online in real time, so anyone can watch," Marc explained.

"So cool," Chloe said. "Are you going to get any shots of the audience on your broadcast?"

Everyone laughed. We knew what Chloe was thinking. There was nothing she loved more than being on camera.

"It's a *basketball game* broadcast," Marc told her. "Not *The Chloe Show*."

Chloe frowned. "Oh, I wasn't talking about me," she insisted. "I just meant that audience shots in general are really interesting."

"Yeah, right," Marc laughed.

"We went out and got new outfits for the game," Marilyn said.

"They're really great," Carolyn added.

"I've got a red shirt and white jeans," Marilyn told us.

"And I've got a white shirt and red jeans," Carolyn added.

"We've got school spirit," Marilyn said.

"Come on, let's hear it," Carolyn added with a giggle.

"It's too bad our school doesn't have a cheerleading squad," Liza told the twins. "You two could be captains. You already have the uniforms."

As my friends kept talking about the basketball game, the film club, Chloe's never-ending quest for stardom, and our school not having a cheerleading squad like the middle schools on TV do, my mind began to drift. *A secret admirer.* I wondered who it could be. The note was typed, so the handwriting didn't give me any clues. And there were no little hints in the text of the note that would give it away, either. My eyes darted around the cafeteria, seeing if there was anyone who seemed to be staring at me. But no one was. Everyone was involved in their own conversations.

Whoever this admirer was, he was really good at keeping it a secret.

I couldn't get him out of my mind. I was still thinking about the note when I got home that afternoon and started my homework. I'm not really all that into boys, or at least *boyfriends* right now — that's more Felicia and Sam's thing. But even as I did my pre-algebra equations, my mind kept drifting back to the note in my pocket.

I had absolutely no idea who my secret admirer was, or what class he and I shared. It could have been any of the classes I had before lunchtime. Sometime during the morning, this guy had managed to slip the note into my notebook. He was obviously very sneaky. But that's part of being a secret admirer, right?

Whoever he was, he'd definitely gotten my attention. I pulled the note out of my pocket and read it again. When I got to the "P.S. I really like you" part, I smiled. It felt really good to be liked. Even by someone I didn't know.

Just then, my cell phone rang. I glanced down at the screen, but I didn't recognize the number on the caller ID. I clicked the answer button anyway. "Hello?" I said.

"Is this Jenny?" a boy on the other end asked. I didn't recognize his voice.

Suddenly, my heart started to pound. This was him. It had to be. "Yes. Who is this?"

"You don't know me," he answered. "But I sure know you. I think you're amazing."

"Um . . . well . . . gee . . . thanks," I stammered. Then I frowned. That hadn't sounded amazing at all. It had sounded kind of stupid, actually.

"That's all I wanted to say," he continued. "I'll see you around, okay?"

"Around where?" I asked, trying to get a clue out of him. But he didn't answer. In fact, he hung up the phone.

Okay, now I was really curious. I had to know who this guy was, and I had to know now! Quickly, I clicked the reply button on my phone, so I could call him back. The phone rang, and rang, and rang. My heart pounded harder and harder with each ring. I could feel myself blushing, even though there was no one in my room (except my pet mice, and I don't have to be embarrassed in front of them). Finally, someone picked up the phone on the other end.

"Joe's Pizza," a man with a deep voice said.

"I . . . um . . . I just got a call from this number," I said nervously. I was kind of thrown by the fact that a grown-up had answered. "And I was trying to figure out who had called me."

"This is a pay phone at a pizza parlor," the man replied. "There are about a zillion kids here right now. How am I supposed to know which one called you?"

A pay phone. My heart sank. I wasn't going to figure out who my secret admirer was. At least not this minute.

"Hey, kid, anything else?" the man asked. "'Cause I gotta get back to the ovens."

"No, no thanks," I said sadly. I hung up the phone.

I obviously wasn't going to discover the identity of my secret admirer today. So there was only one thing left to do. Back to the math homework. *Solve for x in each of these equations . . .* I sighed heavily. I hoped it would be easier to solve for x than it was solving the mystery of *Mr.* X, my secret admirer.

Chapter
FOUR

SOMEHOW, I MANAGED to get through the whole next day of school with just a few thoughts about my secret admirer. Maybe it helped that I was distracted by the pop quiz we had in history. Or maybe it helped that we had a big pep rally to cheer the girls' basketball team on to victory. Or maybe it helped that I didn't get any more notes from him all day. Whatever it was, I didn't think about my secret admirer . . . at least not much.

By the end of the day, I had somehow managed to convince myself that the whole secret admirer thing was probably over. I was just a fleeting crush for some guy, and he'd moved on. Which was why I was really glad I hadn't told anyone about the note or the phone call. I'd have really felt stupid if a day later the secret admirer had changed his mind.

"That was an awesome pep rally!" Felicia said. She and Rachel had stopped by my locker on the way to basketball practice at the end of the day. "I am so totally pumped now!"

"Seriously," Rachel agreed. "Did you hear everyone cheering for us?"

"The whole school is behind you guys," I said, welcoming the distraction of a conversation with two of my best friends.

"Speaking of cheering . . ." Rachel began. A big smile broke across her face.

"Oh, no . . ." Felicia groaned.

"Here it comes," I added. We both recognized the expression on Rachel's face. It was her bad-joke-grin.

"Do you guys know why Cinderella was thrown off the basketball team?" she asked us.

"No. Why?" I asked.

"Why are you encouraging her?" Felicia teased. I shrugged.

"Because she ran away from the ball!" Rachel said, laughing at her own joke. "Get it?"

"We got it, and we're giving it back," Felicia groaned.

But Rachel wasn't about to be deterred. She had plenty more jokes where that had come from. "Do you guys know the difference between a dog and a basketball player?"

Felicia and I shook our heads.

"One drools and the other dribbles!" Rachel exclaimed. Then she started laughing all over again.

I shook my head and opened my locker. I pulled out my history textbook and put it in my backpack. Then I noticed that a small pink envelope had fallen to the floor. My heart began pounding again, and my face turned beet red as soon as I spotted the envelope.

"What's this?" Felicia asked as she picked up the envelope. She took a look at it and grinned. "Hey, do you have a boyfriend I don't know about?" She pointed to the red heart sticker on the envelope.

I sighed. There was no sense hiding it anymore. "I don't know too much about him, either," I said. "He's kind of secretive."

"What's his name?" Rachel asked.

I shrugged. "That's part of the secret." I paused for a minute. "And he's not my boyfriend, either. He's just this guy who sends me notes and calls me. But I don't know who he is."

Felicia's face lit up. "Jenny's got a secret admirer!" she exclaimed.

My eyes opened wide with panic as I caught a glimpse of Addie and her friends just a few lockers away. If they heard about this . . . well . . . I'm not sure what they'd do. But it wouldn't be good. That I knew for sure. "Shhh," I warned Felicia.

"We have to figure out who he is," Felicia whispered.

"Totally," Rachel agreed.

"Why?" I asked.

"So you can have a boyfriend!" Felicia stared at me like I had three heads. "That's why."

"But I don't *want* a boyfriend," I told her.

"You don't know that. What if you like him?" Felicia asked. "What if he's totally your type?"

"I don't have a type," I told her.

"You might," Felicia replied. "You just don't know it yet."

"Besides, if we can figure out who he is, we can satisfy your curiosity," Rachel pointed out. "Admit it — you know you're curious."

I definitely was.

"I know. Let's take a middleschoolsurvival.com quiz!" Felicia exclaimed. "I'm sure they have one that can help you figure out your type."

"Let's?" I repeated. "We're all gonna take it?"

"Well, you want help figuring out this mystery, don't you?" Felicia replied.

I thought about that. I hadn't been too successful on my own. Maybe some help wouldn't be a bad thing. I nodded slowly.

"Good," Felicia declared. "It's settled. Tonight, Rachel and I will call you and we can help you take the quiz. Once we figure out what kind of guy would be perfect for you, we can start looking around for who might be your secret admirer."

I sighed. We didn't even know if my secret admirer *was* my type — if I had a type at all, that is. But taking quizzes was fun. I nodded slowly. "Just don't tell anyone about this, okay, guys?" I pleaded.

Felicia smiled at me. "Not a soul. Your secret about the secret admirer is safe with us."

"A *secret* secret admirer," Rachel said. "How cool is

that? Say did you guys hear the one about the woman who told all her secrets to her parrot?"

Felicia sighed. "No, and we're not going to hear it now. If we're late for practice, we're going to spend most of the championship game on the bench. Coach is getting very strict these days!"

Rachel shrugged. "Okay. I'll tell you another time."

As they walked away, Felicia turned to me and grinned. "This is soooo exciting, Jenny," she said pretty loudly. Or at least loudly enough to get Addie, Sabrina, and Dana's attention. They all looked over at me curiously.

But I didn't say a thing. I didn't even look back toward them. The one thing I didn't need was the Pops finding out about my secret admirer. Those girls gossiped so much. If they got wind of this, my secret admirer wouldn't be a secret any longer.

It turned out the Pops weren't the only ones who couldn't keep a secret. When Rachel and Felicia called me that night, another person was conferenced in on the call – Liza.

"I thought I told you guys not to tell anyone," I said to Felicia and Rachel.

"We need a seventh grader's help in figuring this out," Felicia explained. "What if your secret admirer is a seventh grader?"

"I won't tell anyone, Jenny," Liza assured me.

I knew she wouldn't. Of all my friends, Liza is the most trustworthy. Still, the fact that she was on the phone was proof that I'd broken one of my own middle school rules.

MIDDLE SCHOOL RULE # 24:

IF YOU REALLY WANT TO KEEP SOMETHING SECRET, KEEP IT TO YOURSELF. EVEN YOUR BEST FRIENDS MIGHT LET SOMETHING SLIP ONCE IN A WHILE.

"Let's make a pact that this doesn't go any further than the four of us," Liza suggested. I think she could sense how uncomfortable I was feeling.

"Deal," Rachel agreed.

"Absolutely," Felicia added.

That made me feel a lot better. Now I could focus on the task at hand. "I found one quiz that seemed like what we were looking for," I told my friends. "It's called *Who is Your Prince Charming?*"

"That's exactly what we're trying to figure out!" Felicia said excitedly. "Come on. Read it to us."

I looked at the screen and began to read to my friends.

Who is Your Prince Charming?

When it comes to romance, just what kind of guy is your ideal? Is the boyfriend of your dreams the strong silent type, or the jokester with the twinkle in his eyes? To find out what kind of guy can take you from once upon a time to happily ever after, take this quiz!

1. **Cinderella's prince found her after she left behind a glass slipper. What kind of shoes would your ultimate Prince Charming wear?**

A. A worn-out pair of Vans
B. Designer loafers
C. High-tech running shoes

"What's this supposed to mean?" I wondered out loud. "What do shoes have to do with anything?"

"They must mean something if they're in the quiz," Rachel said. "Otherwise, the question wouldn't be there."

"Josh wears Vans," Felicia pointed out. "They're not worn-out though."

"Josh is *your* boyfriend," Rachel reminded her. "We're focusing on Jenny here."

"I know," Felicia insisted. "I was just saying."

"I guess loafers are kind of cool," I admitted. "But no one in school really wears them."

"Don't worry about that," Liza says. "I don't think the question is really about shoes, anyway. It's more of a way to see what kind of look you go for in a guy."

I sighed and clicked on the letter B. Almost instantly, the next question popped up on the screen.

2. **Every fairy-tale princess gets that one romantic twirl on the dance floor with her prince. What kind of music would your Prince Charming most likely want playing while you two danced?**

A. Emo

B. Pop

C. Rap

"That's easy," I said, clicking on the letter B. "I only listen to pop music."

"Seriously. How do you dance to emo, anyway?" Rachel asked. "It's too angry and depressing."

"That's so true," I agreed as the next question appeared on my monitor.

3. **Where would your ideal Prince Charming's castle most likely be?**

A. In the city, within walking distance of a huge video arcade and an ice-cream parlor

B. By the beach — the perfect spot for boogie boarding and volleyball

C. High up in the mountains near a ton of great hiking

That one took a little thought. "I don't really like the city," I told my friends. "Last time I was there, I was really freaked out by all the people and the subway. The whole sidewalk shook!"

"Well, have you ever gone hiking?" Liza asked.

"At camp," I replied. "It was okay. It got kind of tiring after a while, though."

"How about the beach, then?" Rachel suggested.

"I like the sound of the ocean, but I don't love the sand. It gets in my bathing suit and my ears and stuff."

Felicia sighed. "You're making this so much harder than it has to be," she said.

I knew she was right. But I didn't like thinking about boyfriends and Prince Charmings. At least not as much as she did. It made me uncomfortable. Still, I *did* want to solve the mystery of the secret admirer. So I clicked on the letter C and kept going.

4. Which of these royally romantic gestures would most make you swoon?

A. Having someone write a song for you

B. Receiving a dozen red roses at your desk in school

C. Having someone dance with you in front of the whole school, even though he would rather die than dance in public

"Too bad it doesn't say delivering jelly beans instead of roses," Liza said.

"Yeah, that would be so cool. Addie would totally freak," Rachel said.

"I'm still going to click on B, because it's the closest," I told my friends. "I don't like dancing in public, and writing a song sounds kind of corny, don't you think?"

"It doesn't matter what we think," Liza reminded me. "This is about you. Pick what you think is best."

I did just that. "B it is," I said, clicking the mouse. "Next question."

5. It's a masquerade ball, and everyone is hiding behind a mask. How can you tell which guy is your Prince Charming?

A. He would be the one wearing a funky tie.
B. He would be the best dressed.
C. His muscles would be totally toned.

"I guess I kind of like when a guy dresses nicely," I admitted as I clicked the letter B. "Like the guys in those old black-and-white movies I watch with my mom."

"Ooo, Jenny likes 'em sophisticated," Felicia teased.

I blushed. Even though I was on the phone, that was embarrassing. I was glad no one could see my cheeks.

"That was the last question," I said. "It says my score is four B's and one C."

"What does that mean?" Liza asked me.

I looked down at the chart and read my answer.

Mostly A's: Your ideal Prince Charming is the kind of guy that dances to the beat of his own drum. He's not at all concerned with what others think. He's just happy being himself — and being with you, of course.

Mostly B's: Keep your eyes peeled for a Preppy Prince. When you show up at the ball, you want to know he's dressed up especially for you. There's a little bit of an old time romantic in you — and you want your guy to reflect that.

Mostly C's: Your ultimate Prince Charming is the athletic type. He's the kind of guy who would scale a castle wall to get to you. You just can't resist a guy who's sporty and active.

"Preppy, huh?" Felicia mused out loud. "Who do we know that's prepped out?"

"It doesn't say that the guy who likes me is preppy," I said. Then I stopped. *The guy who likes me.* That sounded so weird.

"Yeah, that's the kind of guy *she* likes," Rachel pointed out. "Her type."

I thought about that. My type. I guess I really did have one.

"But if that's the kind of guy Jenny goes for, then that's probably the kind of guy who would go for her, too," Felicia pointed out.

"Exactly," Liza said. "So tomorrow, we all have to be

on the lookout for preppy guys who have classes or lunch with Jenny."

"Yeah," Felicia agreed. "We should check on the bus, too."

"We don't have any preppy guys on the bus with us, Felicia," I said. "Besides, it's mostly kids we've known for years on that bus. None of them would just suddenly become my secret admirer."

"You never know, Jen," Rachel said. "People change. Things change."

"This is so incredibly romantic," Felicia said with a sigh.

I frowned. That was such a Felicia thing to say. She was all about romance. But having a secret admirer didn't seem particularly romantic to me. It just felt weird.

Chapter
FIVE

"OKAY, SO I'VE MADE A LIST of things we should be on the lookout for," Felicia said as she slid into the seat next to me on the school bus the following morning.

"Shhh . . ." I said, tilting my head back slightly to indicate that Addie was sitting just two seats and across the aisle from us. Not that I had to show her where Addie was sitting. Addie always sat in the same seat on our bus — in the middle, on the right. And she always sat alone. Addie was the only Pop on the bus. There was no way a Pop would ride all the way to school with a non-Pop.

"Right," Felicia agreed, dropping her voice slightly as she pulled a small notebook from her bag. "For starters, there are the loafers. So far, every guy who's gotten on this bus is wearing sneakers — except for Chip Lorimer, who's wearing those black army boots again."

I turned my head to the last seat of the bus where Chip was sitting. At the moment, he and his friend Cory were busy thumb wrestling. Chip was twisting his thumb so hard he was actually sweating. That was just a little too competitive for my taste. I was glad we could cross him off of our potential secret admirer list.

"Whoever your secret admirer is, he has to be neat and organized," Felicia continued. "And into pop music and old movies." She showed me a chart she'd made in her notebook. It had all the characteristics we were looking for, listed neatly.

"It's going to be tough to find someone with all of those characteristics," I said.

"I know," Felicia agreed. "I thought about Marc at one point, because he's into old movies, but he's a total slob. And he wears those same red sneakers every day."

"Marc?" My voice scaled up slightly at the thought. "No way. He's my friend. *Just* my friend."

"I know," Felicia agreed. "I was just showing you how the chart works." She paused for a minute. "You know, I was thinking that maybe it's a good thing you're selling jelly beans at the game," she continued.

I looked at her strangely. "What's so good about selling jelly beans with Addie?" I asked.

"That's not the good part. The good part is you'll be able to see who paid money to have jelly beans delivered. All you'll have to do is check the list and see who bought jelly beans for you. He's got to be one of them."

I nodded. "That's true," I agreed excitedly. Then I stopped. "Unless whoever he is wants them delivered anonymously and doesn't sign his name to the list or the card."

"Hmm. Good point. This is quite a mystery," Felicia said. "Whoever he is, he's good at hiding. I wonder if he's going to send you another note today?"

Out of the corner of my eye, I could see Addie leaning forward slightly. I could tell she was trying to figure out what Felicia and I were whispering about. I grinned slightly. It felt kind of good to see Addie feeling left out and curious for a change.

Still, it was *my* curiosity that was getting the most exercise this week. No matter how many lists Felicia made, or how many faces I scanned at school, I couldn't figure out who my secret admirer was. In fact, the only thing I knew for sure about him was that he was persistent. All week long, I found notes from him — in my book bag, slipped into my locker, and inside my notebooks. You'd be curious too if you'd received a letter like this:

Hi Jenny,
I really liked the green sweater you were wearing today. It made your eyes look even brighter than usual. It's great the way you don't wear makeup like the other girls do.
From,
Your Secret Admirer
P.S. I really like you.

Pretty weird, huh? I didn't know any guys who would ever notice what sweater I was wearing, never mind whether or not I was wearing makeup. At least, I didn't think I did. Anyway, one thing was for sure. Whoever this guy was, he was observant! I had no idea guys ever thought about stuff like that.

Of course, Felicia added that to the list of secret admirer characteristics she, Liza, Rachel, and I were looking for, but it was no help. By Friday afternoon, our list of possible admirers was still blank. And I was down two helpers in our search. It was just Liza and me using the checklist. The only thing Rachel and Felicia could think about was Saturday's big game. Not that I could blame them.

"So are we gonna win, or what?" Marc asked, sticking his video camera in Rachel's face as she and Felicia headed into the gym for practice after school. Marc, Josh, Sam, and I were walking them over to practice before getting on our buses.

"With Felicia and I on the team, we can't lose," Rachel told him.

"That's right," Felicia agreed. "We're the sixth grade super shooters. When we're on the court, we own the game!"

"That was perfect!" Marc said. "I'll edit that into the live broadcast tomorrow. We can play it between quarters."

Rachel gulped. "You're going to put that on the computer?" she asked.

Marc nodded. "Definitely."

Rachel looked over at me. "Is my hair okay?" she asked.

I grinned. Rachel just cut her hair short. It's the first time since first grade that she's had a new hairstyle. She looks really great, but she's kind of paranoid about her bangs.

"You look fantastic," I told her.

"Smashing," Sam added. "I love that 'do, I really do!"

Rachel giggled. "Hey, did I ever tell you guys the one about the hairstylist who . . ."

"Stop right there," Felicia said. "We don't have any time for jokes now. We've got to get to practice."

"But . . ." Rachel began.

"No, let's go," Felicia said firmly. "Once we're champions, you can tell any jokes you want."

Marc grimaced. "That's a dangerous offer," he told her with a teasing laugh.

"One joke," Felicia said, amending her offer.

"That sounds fair," I agreed.

"I don't know — can you stop at just one?" Marc asked Rachel.

Rachel shrugged. "I can try."

Felicia laughed. Then she flashed Josh a smile. "Don't forget, you promised to come over when I get home to help us out."

"I won't forget," Josh assured her.

"Help with what?" I asked him.

"Marc's going to tape the practice," Josh explained. "Then I'm going to go over to watch the tape with Felicia and Rachel to see if there's anything they can do mathematically to improve their game. You know, shoot from a more opportune angle, or pass in a different configuration."

Wow. How amazing were Marc and Josh? They were willing to give up their whole Friday afternoon to help Felicia and Rachel. But I wasn't that surprised. After all, those were the kind of friends I had. The good kind.

Which was more than I could say for Addie. When I arrived at the game on Saturday, the twins had saved a seat for me in the row just behind Liza, Chloe, Josh, and Sam. Good thing, too, because the gym was completely packed. But the Pops hadn't been so thoughtful. And when Addie returned to the bleachers after making sure the eighth grade representatives were all set up at the jelly bean ordering table, she had nowhere to sit. Somehow, it had never occurred to Dana, Claire, Maya, Sabrina, or any of the other Pops to save Addie a seat. And that left Addie with no choice but to climb up to the top of the bleachers and grab a seat on the side, right near a whole group of parents. Talk about being in the wrong place. What could be more horrible than watching a school basketball game with a bunch of grown-ups you don't even know?

Luckily, that wasn't my problem. I was with my pals. And we were psyched! As the team ran out onto the court, we shouted louder than anyone. You could hear us all over the gym. Especially Chloe. When she wants people to pay attention to her, she knows how to do it. She leaped up onto her bleacher seat, and started to cheer for our team, the Joyce Kilmer Middle School Lions.

"Hooray for the Lions, hooray for the Lions! Someone in the crowd yell hooray for the Lions. One, two, three, four! Who are we for? The Lions! That's who!" Then, she sat down and smiled triumphantly into Marc's camera. Obviously, the other members of the film club had thought it would be a good idea to start their broadcast with a cheering fan, and so Marc had taped Chloe's cheer. Sure enough, Chloe'd managed to get herself on the live computer broadcast within the first five minutes of the game. And the smile on Marc's face let me know that it was no surprise to him that Chloe had been able to lead the crowd in a cheer.

As Chloe's cheer ended, Felicia and Rachel looked up into the stands and smiled at us. Then they gave us the "V" for victory sign at exactly the same time.

"Hey, Rachel and Felicia are getting to be like us," Marilyn said.

"Twins on the court," Carolyn agreed.

"They have matching . . ." Marilyn began.

"Red and white uniforms," Carolyn added, finishing her sister's thought.

"I love when you guys do that," Chloe said with a giggle.

"Me, too," I said. "I don't think I'll ever get used to it."

"It's a twin thing," Marilyn and Carolyn said at exactly the same time, and we all began laughing again.

"What time are you going over to work the jelly bean table?" Liza asked me after the laughter died down.

"Not until the fourth quarter," I told her.

"So you have almost a whole game to go before you discover the identity of your secret admirer," she whispered.

"I don't know if he's going to buy jelly beans for me or not."

"What are you two whispering about?" Chloe called over to us.

I could feel my cheeks burning . . . again. When it comes to blushing, *I* could go to the championships. Too bad we didn't have a team for that.

Honk! Just then, the buzzer sounded, and the game began. The two centers leaped up into the air, and Emma Morton, an eighth grader for our team, tapped the ball straight to Felicia. Felicia caught the ball and began dribbling at top speed.

"Go, Felicia! Go!" Josh leaped up and shouted as she raced down the court. Then he looked around, noticed that everyone was staring at him, and sat back down quietly.

I giggled. Josh was so funny. Everyone knew he was Felicia's boyfriend, and he knew everyone knew it. But he still got embarrassed whenever either of them showed that they liked each other — even if it was just by cheering for Felicia at a basketball game.

Felicia was really rocking. But as she got closer to the basket, the girls from Lincoln Middle School closed in on her. Quickly, she passed the ball to Rachel, who easily scored a basket for us.

"Teamwork! Teamwork! Teamwork!" The people on our side of the stands shouted.

"That's all right, that's okay, we're gonna win it anyway," the fans on Lincoln Middle School's side of the stands shouted back. And as if to prove it, they scored a basket. And then another.

But our team wasn't about to just roll over and play dead. Felicia got the ball and passed it to Emma. Emma passed the ball to a seventh grader named Mary, who shot and scored.

"Teamwork! Teamwork! Teamwork!" our side shouted again.

"That's all right, that's okay, we're gonna win it anyway," Lincoln's fans shouted again.

But by halftime, it wasn't clear who was going to win. All through the first half of the game, the lead had been going back and forth. First, we were up by two. Then, Lincoln was up by six. Then, we were up by two again. When the buzzer rang, we were ahead — but by just four points. That's only two baskets. It was clear the Lincoln team was good. They were probably just as good as we were. There was no telling who would win this game.

Unless, of course, you asked Josh. "Did you see the way Felicia passed the ball to Rachel? That was something we worked on last night. If Felicia keeps passing at exactly that speed and angle, they can't miss."

"What if a player from Lincoln gets in the way of the ball?" Chloe pointed out.

Josh shook his head. "We took that into account by varying the height and angle of different passes," he told her.

I grinned. That was Josh. He thought of everything.

And apparently, so had Addie Wilson. As I walked out into the hallway on my way to the cafeteria, I saw a long line of kids waiting to purchase jelly beans for their friends. Once again, I had to admit that Addie knew what she was doing. Everyone wanted to send candy – almost as badly as they wanted to receive it.

As I studied the line of kids, trying to figure out if one of them could be my secret admirer, Addie came strolling over to me. "You're not wearing your 'Buy Jelly Beans for Your Favorite Human Beans' shirt," she said accusingly.

"It's in my backpack," I assured her. "I'll slip it on before I go to the table."

"I wish you would wear it now," Addie said. "It's an advertisement for our project."

"It's just that you gave me a yellow shirt, Addie. And I look terrible in yellow."

"Oh, sorry," Addie apologized, sounding less than sincere. "I thought you'd like a bright sunny color."

Addie knew me long enough to know that when I wore yellow, my skin looked all . . . well . . . yellowy. Come to think of it, that was probably why she'd given it to me instead of the Kelly green one, which one of the seventh grade representatives was now wearing. Kelly green was my favorite color, and Addie knew it. It went with my eyes. Of course, Addie's shirt was sky blue, which made *her* eyes really shine.

"You'd better go back and get it now," Addie said. "We're busier than we thought we'd be. I told Ms. Jaffe we'd open a second table to take care of all the people. You and I will have to work at it. Since it's the sixth grade project, it's only fair that the sixth graders do the most work."

"But I was hoping to watch Rachel and Felicia . . ." I started.

Addie rolled her eyes. "We all have to make sacrifices for the environment," she said.

I would have been perfectly willing to turn the lights off in my room more often, and reuse paper bags. But missing my friends playing in the championship seemed like too much. Still, I knew Addie wasn't going to take no for an answer.

"Okay, I'll be right back," I said reluctantly. Then I turned and headed back toward the gym.

When I got inside, the bleachers were pretty empty. The Pops had disappeared — probably to their girls' room hangout, I figured — and my friends were mostly in the lobby ordering jelly beans or in the cafeteria buying sandwiches. So I just grabbed my backpack and headed for the lobby.

But as I swung the pack over my shoulder, a pencil fell out. That was weird. I was certain I'd zipped it up, but now it was definitely open. I peeked inside to see if anyone had taken anything. (Secretly I hoped they'd taken that hideous yellow T-shirt.) But instead, I saw that someone had put something *in*to my pack instead. There was a big red-and-white heart-shaped sticker stuck to the inside of my book bag.

I peeled the sticker off of the bag and examined it carefully. There was no note or name on the sticker, but I knew right away who it was from. Obviously, my secret admirer had struck again. He was really clever — sticking the sticker in a place where only I would see it.

I held the sticker closer. Mmmm. It smelled like cinnamon. Actually, it was kind of cool.

I was still holding the sticker when I got back out to the lobby, which was a big mistake, because Addie's eyes landed on it immediately. "What's that?" she asked me.

"Oh . . . um . . . nothing," I said, as I shoved the sticker into my backpack and zipped it shut. "Just some dumb scratch-and-sniff sticker."

"Where'd you find it?" Addie asked. "I haven't collected stickers since fourth grade."

I sighed. I already knew that. Back then, Addie and I had shared our sticker collections. We'd traded them and given them as gifts to each other all the time. But of course, Addie had forgotten all about that. Or she was trying to, anyway.

"Yeah, I don't collect them anymore, either," I told her. "It's just a gift from a friend." A friend. Was that exactly true? Could a secret admirer be called a friend? Well, he obviously wanted to be my boyfriend, and a boyfriend is a kind of friend so . . .

"What friend?" Addie pressed.

I wish I knew, I thought to myself. But instead, I changed the subject. "Forget the sticker. We're here to sell candy, right?" I asked, pulling out my bright yellow T-shirt and slipping it over the long-sleeved shirt I was already wearing.

"Yes, we are," Addie said, sitting down at the table, and handing me a pad of paper. "When someone orders jelly beans, write down who they go to. Then give the person buying the jelly beans a card to fill out. We'll attach them to the bags of jelly beans later. Finally, put the money here in this cash box. Got it?"

I rolled my eyes. This wasn't exactly rocket science. But I didn't say anything. I'd be sitting with Addie for a while. Besides, I wanted something from her. So I had to be nice.

"Um . . . Addie?" I said, trying to sound nonchalant.

"What?" she asked, handing a card to an eighth grader and putting two dollar bills into the box.

"Where's the list of jelly beans that have already been ordered?"

A smile crossed Addie's lips. "Do you want to see if anyone's sending you any?"

Darn it. I'd been caught. And even if I'd wanted to hide it, I couldn't, because I was blushing again. I could feel it. Still, all I said was, "I just want to see it, that's all."

"Well, I'm sure at least one of those people you hang around with will send you jelly beans," she said.

I frowned. The way she said *those people* made it sound like we were inferior to her and her friends or something, which we most definitely were not.

"Unless there's someone *special* you want to get candy from," Addie continued, trying to sound all sweet and nice. "Who is it? Tell me. Then I'll check the list."

Oh, no. I wasn't going to tell her anything. There was no way I was going to be fooled into thinking she'd do something just to be nice. I'd fallen for that so many times this year, and I'd always been wrong. Besides, what name was I going to give her?

Luckily, at just that minute, Shane Thomas, a seventh grader, stepped up to the table. "Oh, hi. Do you want to send jelly beans to someone?" I asked.

Shane blushed. "Uh, yeah. I want to send them to Sabrina Rosen."

Addie's ears sure perked up at that one. Sabrina was one of her Pop pals. And the smirk on her face made it clear that since Shane wasn't a Pop, his jelly beans weren't going to mean much to Sabrina.

Still, he wanted to buy them, and I thought that meant we should be nice to him. "Sure," I said, writing Sabrina's name down, and giving him a card. "Just fill this out, pay your two dollars, and we'll make sure she gets them."

But Shane had already seen the look on Addie's face. "Uh, you know what, no thanks. I was just kidding." And with that, he raced off.

"Addie, that wasn't nice," I said.

"What? I didn't say anything," she insisted.

"You didn't have to," I told her.

"You were too pushy, that's all," Addie insisted. Then she smiled at me. "So you never told me. Who are you hoping to get jelly beans from?"

I wasn't telling her, even if I knew. Why was she being so insistent, anyway? Since when did Addie care about anything in my life?

Just then, there was a loud roar coming from the crowd in the gym. The game had probably started again. And someone had just scored. But who? From which team? There was no way to tell from where I was sitting. I sighed. This was going to be a long afternoon. *Really* long.

But even long afternoons end eventually. And finally, Ms. Jaffe came by to tell Addie and I to close up the table. I was thrilled. There were still a few minutes left in the game. At least I'd get some time to cheer my friends to victory.

"Who's winning?" I asked a few minutes later, as I crawled over people to get to the spot where my friends were.

"They are," Marilyn said.

"But only by three points," Carolyn added.

"There's still a minute left on the clock," Chloe told me. "And we're on fire now!"

She wasn't kidding. At just that moment, Felicia stole the ball from a Lincoln team player. She dribbled up the court, stopped, and passed the ball to Rachel. *Swish!* The ball sailed right through the hoop. Suddenly, we were only behind by one point.

"That's her sixth basket in the past five minutes!" Liza told me excitedly. "Rachel's playing her best game ever!"

"Let's go, Lions! Let's go!" Our team's fans cheered.

"Hold the lead!" Their team's fans cheered back. "Hold the lead!"

The screaming got louder and louder, as the Lincoln team got the ball. But I thought the roof was going to blow off of our gym when Rachel stole the ball from them and turned around. And not a minute too soon. We were down to fifteen seconds on the clock.

"I'm free! I'm free!" I heard Felicia scream from a clear spot in front of the basket. Or make that *saw* her scream. I couldn't actually hear anything except the cheers of the people around me. I could only see Felicia's mouth moving and her arms flailing in the air.

"Ten, nine, eight . . ." the crowd began counting down.

As they reached five, Rachel stopped in her tracks, right near the center line of the court. She lifted the ball and looked around the court. And then, she shot it right at the basket.

It was like the entire population of the gym was holding its breath as the ball soared through the air, coming closer and closer to the basket. The ball went up in a perfect arc, coming down just over the basket.

I glanced up at the clock. Three . . . two . . .

The ball hit the rim, teetered around for a moment, and then . . . fell off to the side. The buzzer went off. Lincoln had won the game. Rachel looked like she was about to cry. So did the rest of the team. All except Felicia. She just looked mad. Really mad!

"You BALL HOG!" she shouted. "You lost the game for us."

Rachel turned around and glared at her. "I can't believe you just called me that," she screamed back.

"Believe it!" Felicia yelled. "Because that's what you are! A BALL HOG!"

"Yeah, well, you've got horrible aim. If you hadn't missed those free throws in the second half, I wouldn't have had to shoot that last basket."

People were turning around and staring at them. It seemed like everyone heard the argument. And whoever didn't would be able to hear it later — because Marc had caught the whole thing on camera. Rachel and Felicia's fight was being broadcast live on the Internet!

Chapter
SIX

"THIS IS BAD," Marilyn said at lunch on Monday.

"*So* bad," Carolyn agreed.

"I don't think they've spoken to each other since Saturday," Chloe pointed out.

"That's what Felicia told me on the bus," I said. "She even said she wouldn't go to the team dinner if Rachel was going."

"Is she?" Sam asked.

I shrugged. "I don't know. I haven't seen Rachel yet today."

"I have," Chloe said. "And she says she won't go if Felicia does. Rachel is majorly mad. Not that I blame her."

"You *can't* blame Felicia," Josh said.

"I can't?" Chloe asked indignantly.

"No," Josh insisted. "Rachel lost the game for the entire school with that show-off shot of hers."

"Not exactly," Marc pointed out. "The game was pretty tight at that point. And like Rachel pointed out, Felicia did miss those two free throws earlier in the fourth quarter. We wouldn't have needed Rachel's basket at all if she'd made her free throws."

"But the point is we *did* need those points, and at least Rachel tried," Marilyn said.

"Tried and missed," Carolyn pointed out. "If she'd just passed the ball to Felicia . . ."

"Felicia might have missed," Marilyn insisted, "again."

"WHAT?!" Josh and Carolyn shouted out at once.

I stared at them. Now that was weird. Usually, it was Marilyn and Carolyn who were in unison. But today, the twins were on opposite sides.

So were Marc and Josh. "Look, dude, just because Felicia's your girlfriend doesn't mean she's always right. You're a smart guy. You know she should have made those shots. You're the one who taught her all about what angles she should shoot from in the first place." He paused for a minute. "Hey, maybe *you're* the one who's at fault. Maybe it was your geometry lesson that made Felicia screw up so badly."

Josh's eyes got small and squinty. He took a deep breath. "She did not screw up. And neither did I. You just don't know what you're talking about. You're a moron!"

I gulped. This was getting bad. Marc didn't take being called names well. (Then again, who does?) I was almost relieved when Josh grabbed his tray and got up. "I'm going to the library!" he declared.

Wow! This was spiraling totally out of control. In fact, everyone seemed to have a point of view about who'd actually lost the game. By mid-afternoon, I started to notice people in the halls with writing on their arms. Some had written TEAM RACHEL! Others had written TEAM FELICIA!

That was bad enough. But what made it worse was that Rachel and Felicia's friends were doing it, too. Josh, of course, had a big red TEAM FELICIA on his arm. So did Carolyn and Sam. On the other hand, Chloe had proudly declared herself part of TEAM RACHEL, as had Marilyn and Marc. In fact, it seemed only Liza and I were staying neutral.

Well, actually, Liza, *the Pops*, and I were neutral. Addie and her crowd of friends had a made a point of not placing themselves on a team. It was easy to figure out why. They didn't like Rachel *or* Felicia. They didn't like anyone who wasn't a Pop. And they certainly weren't going to be part of any campaign that took attention away from them.

That meant that since I wasn't taking sides in the Felicia/Rachel war, and the Pops weren't either, the Pops and I were sort of on the same side. Liza found that really weird when I pointed it out to her at the end of the school day.

"This is the first time I've ever agreed with the Pops on anything," Liza said. "But this whole war over who actually lost the game is the stupidest thing in the world."

I nodded. "I know. And it's really getting bad."

Just then, Marilyn and Carolyn walked by. Well, stomped by, actually. You could tell they were angry just by the way they were making their way down the hall. For starters, they weren't looking at each other. And for another, they were no longer finishing each other's sentences the way they usually do.

"Jenny, what are you doing after school today?" Carolyn asked me. "'Cause I was thinking maybe I could go home with you. The less time I spend with her, the better, you know?"

Marilyn laughed. "Oh, like that's really going to hurt my feelings." She turned to Liza. "You want to come over to my house for a while? We could hang out. *Just the two of us.*"

Liza and I exchanged glances. We knew that neither of us could spend the afternoon with Marilyn or Carolyn. Or any of our friends for that matter. It would be like we were choosing sides. And neither of us wanted to do that.

But our friends sure wanted us to.

"You guys are going to have to decide who was right and who was wrong sometime," Marilyn said.

"Come on," Carolyn argued. "We all know the answer to that."

"You apparently don't," Marilyn countered.

"Actually, Jenny and I are going to my house this afternoon," Liza said, before the argument could get any worse.

"Well, maybe the three of us could hang out," Carolyn suggested. "You, Jenny, and me."

Liza shook her head. "Jenny and I've kind of planned this to be just the two of us," she said. "Maybe another time." Then she looked at her wrist. "Wow. Look how late it is. We've got to get going to the bus."

As she pulled me away, I looked at her and laughed. "You're not wearing a watch," I reminded her.

Liza shrugged. "As long as they didn't notice, it's fine."

"They were too busy glaring at each other to notice," I said with a sigh.

"I know. This is getting out of hand," Liza agreed.

"Today in history class, Chloe and Sam refused to sit in the same row," I told her.

Liza shook her head with dismay. "Did you see Marc and Josh at lunch? I thought Marc was going to pour his milk over Josh's head."

I nodded. "It was a good thing Josh got up and left the table."

Liza frowned. "I never thought this would happen to us. I mean, we're not the Pops."

I knew what she meant. The Pops were always getting in fights and turning on one another. But our friends never did. Until now, anyway.

Just then, Addie came racing up to us on the way to the parking lot. She was followed closely by Sabrina, Dana, and Maya. "Jenny, you've got to do something about Felicia and Rachel. This is a total mess. They can't keep fighting like this. It's not right."

I stared at her with surprise. Addie looked genuinely upset about what had happened between my friends. That was totally not like her.

On the other hand, Addie, Rachel, Felicia, and I had all gone to elementary school together. So Addie knew better than most people how close Rachel and Felicia had always been. Almost as close as Addie and I had been. Maybe it really did upset her that two people who'd been so close were fighting.

"I mean, you wouldn't believe how many people want to cancel their jelly bean deliveries to people because they're on different sides of this thing," Addie continued.

I rolled my eyes. Then again, maybe not. It had been too much to hope that Addie actually cared about someone else for a change.

"I keep telling them there are no refunds, but no one's giving up," Addie continued. "And people are refusing to order any more jelly beans. My whole environment project is going to fall apart."

"First of all, Addie, it's the sixth grade project, not *your* project," I reminded her.

"Well, I'm in charge," she insisted.

"Yeah, she's in charge," Maya echoed.

"Whatever," I said, not wanting another argument. I'd heard enough of those today. "The thing is, I can't control Felicia and Rachel, or anyone else in the school."

"But someone has to do something," Addie snarled.

"Well, you're in charge," I reminded her. "Maybe *you* can convince them to make up."

Addie's face turned positively purple with anger. "Thanks for nothing!" she said as she stormed off.

As soon as Addie was out of earshot, I turned back toward Liza. "Addie's right about one thing," I told her. "This is a total mess. Felicia and Rachel joined the basketball team so they could have an after school activity to do together, and now it's totally pulled them apart. Not to mention everyone else."

"Well, at least *we're* not fighting," Liza said with a smile. "We can hang out all afternoon."

"Hooray for Team Us!" I answered, returning her grin.

Chapter
SEVEN

"MY MOM SAID TO CALL HER when we got to your house,"
I told Liza as we headed into her living room a little while
later. I reached into the front pocket of my book bag
for my phone. Instead, I pulled out a piece of thick, red
cardboard in the shape of a heart. There was a message
glued to it.

```
To Jenny,
Your lips are red,
Your eyes are green.
You're the coolest girl,
I've ever seen.
From,
Your Secret Admirer
P.S. I really like you.
```

Wow. I'd been so caught up in the whole Rachel-Felicia
drama, I'd almost forgotten about the mystery man in my
life. But he obviously wasn't about to let that happen! I
frowned slightly. I could add another clue to our list now.
He wasn't much of a poet. It was actually pretty lame.

"Another note from your secret admirer?" Liza asked me.

Just then a small voice piped up from behind the couch. "Jenny has a secret admirer?"

"Spencer, Mom told you not to snoop," Liza told her younger brother.

"I wasn't snooping," he told her. "I was just hanging out."

"Behind the couch where you can't be seen?" Liza asked him.

"Uh-huh."

Liza didn't believe him, and neither did I. But he wasn't my little brother. I couldn't say anything. But Liza could.

"It's a big house," Liza told him. "Find another place to hang out, *please*."

Spencer ignored her and focused his attention on me. "Having a secret admirer sounds fun," Spencer said. "Who's yours?"

"It wouldn't be a secret if she knew that," Liza reminded him.

"Oh, yeah," Spencer agreed. "Are his notes all mushy because he likes you?"

I thought about that for a minute. "Not so much mushy. Just kinda nice. And sometimes he gives me little presents," I added, thinking of the sticker that had been stuck to the inside of my bag during the basketball game.

"Does he want to be your boyfriend?" Spencer asked.

I blushed. "Well . . . I . . ."

"Come on, Spence," Liza said. "Go hang out in your room. This isn't any of your business."

"Jenny's my friend, too," he insisted.

I smiled at him. Spencer could be a pain, but he was kind of cute, for a third grader. "Sure I am," I said, not wanting to hurt his feelings. "But Liza and I have some middle school stuff to talk about now. I can hang out with you a little bit later."

Liza and I watched as Spencer left the room in search of something to do. "Sorry about that," she said, once he was out of earshot. "He just wants to hang out with us because we're older."

I grinned at her. "It's okay," I said. "He's pretty funny."

"Sometimes he can be," Liza agreed. She glanced down at the card in my hand. "Who do you think he is?"

I shrugged. "I don't have a clue," I said. "He's very careful. I have no idea when he slips these things into my bag."

"I wonder if he's on Team Felicia or Team Rachel," Liza joked.

I rolled my eyes. "I hope he's on neither. That's all I'd need."

"I wish there was some way we could get Rachel and Felicia to just talk to each other," Liza said.

"That would be nice," I agreed, "because frankly, I'm tired of hearing everyone talk about who they think really lost the game. All I've done today is listen to my friends complain about each other. Honestly, I feel like I'm not even listening to them anymore. I'm just pretending."

"Don't be silly," Liza assured me. "You're a great listener. And everyone appreciates it."

I smiled. Liza always knew exactly what to say to make me feel better.

"Hey, you guys want some brownies?" Spencer asked as he ran in from the kitchen. "They're the good kind – with the chocolate icing!"

Liza sighed. It was clear that she didn't want to be having a snack with her little brother right now. But I had promised to hang out with him. And besides, I was kind of hungry.

"Sounds yummy," I said, getting up from the couch.

I turned toward Liza. She shrugged and mouthed the words, "I'm sorry."

I smiled and mouthed back, "It's okay." And it really was. I don't know if it's because I'm an only child, or because Spencer was really a nice kid, but I didn't mind spending time with him. Besides, he was acting much more grown-up than my friends at school were lately.

Liza had been really nice to tell me I was a good listener and all, but the idea that I wasn't really paying attention to what my friends were saying to me had nagged at me all afternoon. I tried to be a good friend all the time, not just when it was convenient for me. And the idea that I wasn't being very helpful was kind of upsetting.

Was it possible that I wasn't as good of a listener as I thought I was?

I wasn't surprised to find that there was a quiz that could answer that question on middleschoolsurvival.com. That's why it was my favorite site. It had the answers — or at least the quizzes with the answers — to everything!

How Good a Listener Are You?

When your friends are speaking to you, you hear them — but are you really listening to what they're saying? Take this quiz, and find out just how good a listener you really are.

1. **Your BFF comes running over to tell you something important. But just as she opens her mouth, your cell phone rings. It's that guy you've been crushing on all month. What do you do?**

   A. Nothing — let him ring through to voice mail.
   B. Pick up the phone, but only speak long enough to tell him you'll have to call him back.
   C. Promise your pal you'll talk to her later, and then take his call.

At first I thought I could knock C off my list right away. My initial reaction was that ditching your friend because a guy was calling was really wrong. But then I thought about my secret admirer. If he called, would I be so quick to let him ring through to my voice mail? Probably not. So I compromised, and clicked the letter B. That seemed the most truthful answer.

2. **You walk into the girls' room and see your friend there. It's pretty obvious from her makeup-stained face that she's been crying, but when you ask her about it, she tells you she's fine. Do you . . .**

   A. Nod understandingly, and tell her you're here to listen if she needs you?
   B. Take her at her word, and then hurry off before you're late for class?
   C. Tell her you know better, and gently convince her to tell you what's up? After all, you can't help her with her problem if you don't know what it is.

   I studied the choices carefully. Wow. This was a tough one. I mean obviously I would know something was really wrong, and I would definitely want to help, so B wouldn't be my choice. On the other hand, I'm not very confrontational. And I don't think I could have forced any of my friends to tell me what was up before they wanted to. So I eliminated C. I figured my best choice had to be A, so that was the one I clicked.

3. **Your best friend has just called to talk to you about a really embarrassing thing that happened today — her pants split in the middle of gym class. But you have something really exciting to tell her about you and that new boy in your math class. How much give and take does your chat have?**

A. You listen for a while, and then interrupt to tell her that you don't think split pants is that big of a deal. Then you let her go back to what she was saying. You can tell her your story when she's through venting.

B. You listen to everything she has to say before responding.

C. You insist on telling your story first. A cute boy is obviously more important than a pair of ripped pants. Anyone can see that, right?

Finally, an easy question. B. Definitely B. I always let my friends finish what they're saying — which isn't always easy, especially on days like today when people are saying all kinds of really mean things about one another.

4. **Your friend is telling you a story about her new puppy, Patches. She's going into great detail about what life with a pup is like. Where are you looking while you're listening to your friend?**

A. I usually look the person in the eye during a conversation, although sometimes I might glance at my watch or fidget.

B. I tend to get distracted and look away.

C. I make a real effort to keep eye contact with the person who is speaking.

I thought about that for a while. I knew the answer that would make me the best listener was C. Eye contact with the other person helps you listen to what they're saying.

But there was no sense just giving the computer the answers I knew it was looking for. I had to be honest so I could find out the truth about myself. And the truth is, even though I try to look the person in the eye, sometimes I do glance away at a clock, or the floor, or the kid down the hall. Not often, but enough to make my answer A instead of C.

5. Your friend tells you about a new lipstick she just bought. It's the kind that's supposed to stay on all day, except hers stayed on a lot longer. In fact, she can't get it off! How do you react?

A. Compare her story with a worse one of your own, like the time an allergic reaction to your mascara made your eye swell shut.

B. Try to help her find a solution to her lip drama by suggesting she call the makeup company and ask them for a suggestion.

C. Change the subject since you don't wear makeup and can't relate.

Okay, I could click C, because I don't really wear makeup. But I don't usually change the subject unless there's going to be an argument among my friends. (I told you, I'm not very confrontational.) And I'm not the kind of person who likes to compete. I'm more of a problem solver. So I clicked the letter B.

That was the end of the quiz. I waited a moment until the computer added up my score.

1. A. 1 point   B. 2 points   C. 3 points
2. A. 2 points   B. 3 points   C. 1 point
3. A. 2 points   B. 1 point   C. 3 points
4. A. 2 points   B. 3 points   C. 1 point
5. A. 2 points   B. 1 point   C. 3 points

You have a total of 8 points.

What does that mean? Listen up and you'll find out.

5-8 points: Congratulations! You are an excellent listener. Your friends can surely tell that you're interested in their lives and concerned about them. And because you are, chances are they will be there for you when you need them to listen.

9-12 points: This is where most people fall on the listening scale. For the most part, you are making an effort to really hear and understand what your friends are telling you, but sometimes you can get a little preoccupied with your own stuff. Try to work a little harder to stay focused on the topic at hand.

13-15 points: Your listening skills need some help. You may be taking part in the conversation, but you're not hearing what your friends are telling you. Try to focus on honing your listening skills. It's important that you let the people you care about most know that you are sincerely hearing what they're telling you, and that you want to help.

Wow! I was a better listener than I thought. That was pretty cool. But considering all the stuff I'd had to listen to today, I was still going to have to work hard to keep my listening skills in top form. I wanted to be the best friend I could be — to everyone, no matter what team they were on!

As if on cue, my cell phone rang. I checked the caller ID. Felicia. I took a deep breath before I answered. I knew it was going to take all of my listening skills to get through this conversation.

"Hey, Leesh," I greeted her.

"Hi, Jenny," Felicia replied. "I missed you on the bus after school today. I saved you a seat, but you weren't there."

My listening skills told me that even though Felicia hadn't actually asked me a question, her tone of voice made it clear she wanted to make sure I hadn't gone home with Rachel or one of her supporters.

"I went home with Liza," I assured her.

"Oh," the relief in her voice was obvious. "What did you guys do?"

"We hung out and danced around to some new songs she'd downloaded, ate brownies, and played Crazy Eights with her brother Spencer. Just typical stuff."

"Sounds fun," Felicia said. "I don't have a lot to do since the season ended."

"Yeah, I guess it's kind of a let down after all the excitement," I replied.

Oh man, was that the wrong thing to say. The anger in Felicia's voice was clear as she spoke. "Well, it didn't have to be. If we'd won the championship then we'd be having all kinds of celebrations. But thanks to that ball hog . . ."

I was actually glad when I got another call. At first, I considered hanging up on Felicia to take the call, but then I remembered the quiz. What was it I'd said I'd do if someone called when I was talking to a good friend? Oh yeah, pick up the call just for a second and tell the person on the other end I'd call them back after I'd finished my other conversation.

"Hold on a sec, Felicia," I said. "I've got another call, but I'll tell whoever it is that I'll call back."

I put Felicia on hold and clicked on the other call.

"Hi, Jenny."

I gulped. It was Rachel on the other end. For a second, I felt guilty, like I was being unfaithful. But to who? To Rachel, for being on the other line with Felicia? Or to Felicia, for being on this line with Rachel?

Either way, I was being ridiculous. For one thing, I hadn't called either of them. And for another, this was their fight, not mine. "Hey, Rachel," I said. "Listen, can I call you back in a few minutes? I'm sort of on the other line."

"With who?" Rachel asked suspiciously.

"Um . . . my cousin, Michael," I told her. I frowned. I

hated lying to Rachel, but it seemed the easiest way to avoid an argument.

"Oh, okay. Then I'll talk to you in a few minutes."

As I clicked the phone to go back to Felicia, I sighed heavily. I was suddenly exhausted. Who knew that someone else's war could be so tiring?

"Okay, we've got to do something quick," I told Liza during our phone conversation about a half hour later. "I'm tired of being stuck in the middle of those two."

"You and me both," Liza said. "They're both trying to make me vow to be on their side of the argument, which is ridiculous. They're both wrong."

"Exactly," I agreed. "I liked it better when we all had a common enemy — the Pops."

Liza laughed. "The enemy of my enemy is my friend," she said. "Yeah, those were the good old days."

"Actually, it was only three days ago," I reminded her. "It just seems like years."

Just then, the call waiting on my cell phone clicked again. "Oh, no," I groaned.

"Is it a member of Team Felicia or Team Rachel?" Liza asked.

I moved the phone from my ear and looked at the caller ID. Addie. Oh, no. She probably just wanted to complain about how the absolute destruction of my middle school world was affecting *her*. There was absolutely no way I was taking her call now. It was one thing to answer the call waiting when there was a friend on the other end. But I wasn't about to stop talking to Liza for a second for one of the Pops.

I'm not *that* good of a listener!

Chapter
EIGHT

WHEN I BOARDED THE BUS the next morning, I knew Felicia would have a seat saved for me. For a second, I considered sitting somewhere else, just in case Rachel heard that I was sitting with Felicia and figured I was on her side. But then again, on the other hand, if I didn't sit with Felicia, *she* would think I was on Rachel's side. *Grrrrr.* This was getting totally out of hand.

In the end, I sat down next to Felicia. There was no way out of it. Addie boarded the bus right after me, and she went right to her regular seat. She smiled as she passed by. At least with her mouth, she smiled. Her eyes were more like glaring. It was like she was broadcasting a message to me: *You'd better fix this.*

Believe me, if I could have, I would have. And not for Addie's stupid jelly bean project, either. More for my own sanity. But Felicia didn't want to talk about her fight with Rachel. She wanted to talk about me.

"So, did you get anything from him yesterday?" Felicia wondered.

I didn't have to ask who she was talking about. "Yeah. A poem."

"Ooo, a poem!" Felicia squealed, a little too loudly. "How romantic."

"Not really," I told her. "It was kinda goofy."

"Still," Felicia insisted. "He wrote you a *poem*. Did it give you any clues?"

I shook my head. "Nope. I still can't figure out a thing. Especially how he manages to slip this stuff into my backpack."

"This guy is amazing. He's taken being a secret admirer to a whole new level," Felicia said. "You've got to *admire* that."

"Ouch," I said with a grimace. "That was a bad joke. Almost as bad as . . ." I stopped myself. I was about to say as bad as one of Rachel's, but I couldn't for obvious reasons. Still, Felicia knew what I had in mind. She nodded quietly and looked out the window.

A few minutes later, we pulled up at school. Addie dashed off the bus at top speed and headed right into the waiting arms of the Pops, who had gathered near the school. Felicia and I followed close behind. A moment later, Josh and Carolyn came over to us.

"Well, hi, Jenny," Carolyn said with a knowing grin.

Uh-oh. Just as I'd suspected. People were starting to think I had taken Felicia's side in the fight. "Uh, hi," I answered her cautiously. "Felicia and I just got off the bus. . . ."

"Where we were sitting *together*," Felicia added pointedly.

"Mmm . . . yeah," I said. "But now I have to go do something in the library. So, uh, I'll see you guys later. Yeah, well. Bye." And with that, I hurried off toward the school.

But I didn't get far. As I sailed past the sea of Pops standing by the school door, I was greeted by a loud chorus of giggles.

"Jenny has a secret admirer," Addie said loudly.

"If I was her admirer, I'd keep it a secret, too," Dana told her.

Oh, no! Addie had overheard my conversation with Felicia on the bus. This was my worst nightmare — and it was happening in the daytime. I tried to hurry into the building, but Addie and Dana blocked my path.

"He sends her love poems," Addie said. "I heard them talking about it."

"Poems," Maya said. "How corny."

"He's probably some geek," Sabrina suggested.

"I knew there was a reason you wanted to check that jelly bean delivery list," Addie said to me.

"No . . . that's not it," I murmured feebly.

"Of course it is," Addie insisted.

"I can just see the card now," Claire said. "Dear Jenny, you're the weirdest girl I've ever seen. When I look at you, my face turns green. From your secret admirer."

The Pops burst into a fresh chorus of giggles.

"And don't forget — P.S. I really like you." Dana laughed so hard she snorted.

My eyes opened wide. "How did you know about that?" I asked her.

The Pops stopped laughing. They stared at the ground. Addie punched Dana in the side.

"Oops," Dana murmured quietly.

Oh, man! The nightmare had just gotten worse. There was no way Dana could have known about what was written in my letters . . . *unless she'd helped write them.* "It was you!" I shouted at the crowd of silent Pops. "You guys did this!"

"I don't know what you're talking about, Jenny," Addie said, but she was a lousy liar. The look on her face told me she definitely *did* know what I was talking about.

"So I guess you won't be getting any jelly beans after all," Dana told me. She smiled at her friends. "At least *we'll* be buying them for *one another*. We don't need secret admirers."

So that was it! They must have overheard my friends and I talking about how the Pops weren't going to get as much candy as they thought because the only people who really liked the Pops were the Pops.

Unless they had secret admirers. That's what I'd said. I'd actually been the one to give them the idea! How ironic was that? Obviously, I'd made them mad. Mad enough to do something this mean.

Nah. Who was I kidding? The Pops didn't need an excuse to be mean. That's just how they were. As I pushed my way toward the school I blinked my eyes a few times, and tried to keep another unwritten middle school rule in my head.

MIDDLE SCHOOL RULE #25:
NEVER LET YOUR ENEMIES SEE YOU CRY. THAT ONLY LETS THEM WIN.

Unfortunately, number 25 is an especially tough rule to keep. And by the time I reached the school building, the tears were flowing. They were fierce tears, too — the salty, burning kind. It really hurt. And I was burning up inside, too. I felt like my whole world was falling apart around me, and there was nothing I could do about it.

That afternoon, I went home with Liza again. It seemed as though her house was a safe haven. There were no Pops on her bus, and by going home with her I didn't have to face a ride home with Addie laughing at me. And as long as Liza and I were together, I didn't have to worry about one friend thinking I liked her better than another. Liza and I were neutral, like Switzerland.

"It all makes sense now," I said, as Liza and I sat on her bed. "Addie and Dana are in a lot of my classes, which gave them plenty of opportunities to slip things into my backpack when I wasn't looking."

"Did they actually admit that?" Liza wondered, stunned.

I shook my head. "No. They never own up to what they do. But they didn't deny it, either."

"But what about that phone call from the pizza parlor?"

I shrugged. "They probably asked one of those jerky boys they hang around with to do it."

"Are you disappointed about not having a secret admirer?" Liza asked me.

I thought about that. I didn't really want a boyfriend. Not yet, anyway. Still, it had been kind of cool thinking that someone out there liked me. "Not disappointed. More like embarrassed and . . ."

But before I could finish my sentence, Liza and I heard some rustling noises coming from the hallway. Someone was outside her door — listening!

Liza tiptoed over to the door, staying extra quiet, so the person on the other side would be totally surprised. Then she threw open the door, knocking the eavesdropper on his rear end. "Spencer!" Liza exclaimed. "You were spying again."

"No I wasn't," he insisted.

"Then what were you doing outside my door?" Liza asked. I could tell she was struggling to keep from getting really furious with her younger brother.

"I was going to the bathroom," he told her.

"The bathroom is in the other direction," Liza pointed out.

"Oh, yeah."

"So if you've gotta go . . . then go," Liza suggested firmly, but not too meanly. Liza just can't be mean, even when she's angry.

Spencer obviously didn't have to go that badly. "So can you get another secret admirer?" he asked me as he walked into Liza's room.

I shrugged. "I guess. But I don't think that will happen." I sighed.

"Jenny, come on. It's no big deal. The Pops do mean stuff to people all the time. And then they get bored and move on to something else," Liza told me.

I knew what Liza was talking about. When she'd won a big history contest at our school, the Pops were so jealous they'd tried to convince everyone that Liza had cheated. Which she hadn't, of course. Liza was too honest to do something like that.

Liza was right. The Pops had gotten over that. And after they'd finished making her life miserable, they'd moved on. Unfortunately, they'd moved on to me. Suddenly, those burning, angry tears began to form in my eyes again.

"Jenny, don't cry," Spencer said. "I hate when people cry."

Liza smiled kindly at Spencer. I knew how she felt. It was genuinely impossible to stay mad at the kid for very long. He really was sweet.

"Come on. Let's all go down to the kitchen and get some ice cream," Liza urged both of us. "There's no problem that a little rocky road can't solve."

The next morning, as I waited at the bus stop, Addie made a point of staying as far away from me as possible. But not because she was ashamed of what she'd done to me — Addie could always justify her actions, no matter how horrible. No, Addie was keeping her distance because my backpack stank. It smelled like a mix of flowers and spices. I'd have moved away from it, too, if I could have, but unfortunately, I had to carry it.

"What is that stink?" Addie finally demanded.

I glared at her, my eyes shrinking into angry slits. "You know very well what it is, Addie. It's perfume."

"How would I know that?" she demanded.

"Because you're the one who slipped that little sample container of it into my backpack. Last night, the plastic tube opened up and spilled all over my stuff. I can't get rid of the stink, and my mom hasn't had time to get me a new backpack yet." I took a deep breath. "Come on, Addie, cut it out already. I know it's you guys. The joke's over."

Addie looked at me strangely. "Perfume? We never gave you perfume."

Now it was *my* turn to look at *her* strangely. She actually seemed to be telling the truth. Which could only mean one thing . . . maybe I really *did* have a secret admirer.

Chapter

NINE

AS I SAT THERE ALL ALONE at my lunch table, I felt as bad as I had on the first day of school, when I'd been so embarrassed to be seen alone that I'd eaten in the phone booth. But I wasn't embarrassed this time. Everyone knew I had friends. What was upsetting was that all of my of friends hated one another.

As I looked across the room, I could see Josh, Carolyn, and Sam (Team Felicia) sitting at a corner table, eating lunch. From time to time they would shoot angry glances at a table where Chloe, Marc, and Marilyn (Team Rachel) were eating their lunch. It was not a pretty sight.

Oh, and then there were the Pops. They were at their usual table. But the only person they kept looking over at was me. They were staring and whispering. Surely, Addie had told them about the perfume and my *real* secret admirer. They were obviously amazed.

Come to think of it, so was I. Just when I'd adjusted to the fact that there was no mystery man in my life, it turned out there was. And so far, all I knew about him was that he had horrible taste in perfume. That stink was still following me everywhere.

"Whoa, you smell like you took a bath in perfume," Liza said as she sat down across from me at the lunch table.

I stared at her for a minute in surprise. It wasn't usually like Liza to say something like that. But the stench was pretty bad.

"It's a gift from my new secret admirer," I told her.

Liza rolled her eyes. "Are the Pops at it again?"

I shook my head. "Addie looked genuinely shocked when I told her that the perfume sample she slipped into my backpack had opened. The Pops didn't do this. I think this time I really have a secret admirer."

"Perfume sample?" she asked.

I nodded. "It looked like a mini plastic test tube. Unfortunately, it wasn't sealed very tightly."

"Was there a note?" she asked.

I shook my head. "Nope. All I found was the empty sample container. And, of course, the perfume, which is now all over my bag and my notebooks. My mom's taking me out tonight to replace the backpack. I've been handing in scented homework all day, though."

Liza sniffed at the air again. "I recognize that smell," she said slowly. "It's really familiar."

"Maybe you smelled it in a magazine or something," I suggested.

Liza shook her head. "No. I know someone who wears that scent."

"Ooo. If we can figure out who that is, maybe we'll have a clue about my secret admirer," I suggested excitedly.

Liza nodded slowly. "I think I already know who your secret admirer might be."

"Really, tell me? Is he a seventh grader like you?" I asked excitedly. "Do I know him?"

Liza shook her head. "No. He's not a seventh grader. But you know him, all right."

"Spencer, come here," Liza called out as we walked into her house after school that afternoon.

Spencer came out of the kitchen. He'd obviously just finished having his after-school snack, because when he saw me, he smiled brightly, flashing a milk moustache. "Hi, Jenny," he said.

"Hey, Spence," I replied.

"Spencer, we have to ask you something," Liza said quietly. "And we want you to be really honest when you answer."

"Okay," Spencer agreed.

"Did you take one of Mom's perfume samples and put it in Jenny's backpack yesterday?" Liza asked him.

Spencer looked away and kicked at the ground. He didn't speak. He didn't have to. The red blush in his cheeks said it all.

My eyes popped open wide. My new secret admirer was Spencer. He looked so cute and vulnerable standing there that I couldn't even be disappointed. "Thank you for the perfume," I told him. "That was very nice of you."

"How'd you figure out it was me?" he asked. "I didn't sign my name or anything. I just gave you a present."

"I didn't figure it out," I assured him. "You were very secretive."

"Then what happened?" Spencer wondered.

"It's Mom's perfume," Liza told him. "I recognized the smell, and figured you took one of the samples from her travel bag."

"Do you think Mom will be angry that I took it?" Spencer asked nervously.

Liza shook her head. "The samples are free. Mom just uses them for traveling. She won't be angry. It's a good thing you didn't take the big bottle on her makeup table, though."

I nodded. She wasn't kidding. And not just because the big bottle was expensive. The little sample had totally stunk up everything I owned. I couldn't imagine what I would have smelled like if a whole bottle of perfume had opened in my bag.

Spencer breathed a heavy sigh of relief. Then he looked up at me. "Did you like my present?" he asked eagerly.

I nodded. "It was really nice."

"So can I be your secret admirer?"

I laughed. "You know what? I don't like secrets," I told him. "Or admirers. What I really want is a good friend. How about you and I just agree to be good friends?"

"You mean you'll hang out with me when you come home with Liza?" he asked.

I nodded. "Sure. But sometimes Liza and I might want to do girl things."

Spencer thought about that. "I guess that's okay," he said. "I don't like doing girl things anyhow." And with that, he ran off toward the kitchen.

"That wasn't too bad," I said as we watched him leave.

"You were great with him," Liza told me. "Only now you're going to find yourself playing an awful lot of checkers and Twister. Those are his new obsessions."

I laughed. "I kinda like Twister," I admitted. "Addie, Felicia, Rachel, and I used to play all the time in elementary school. Addie always won, of course . . ." I grew quiet, remembering how much easier things seemed to be back then.

"That really stinks," Liza said, reading my mind.

"Not as bad as my backpack," I joked.

Liza giggled. "I meant, Addie always winning, you know."

I nodded. "I know. Addie doesn't take losing well. Right now I have her on my back about the slowdown in jelly bean sales," I told her. "Like it's all my fault or something. What am I supposed to do about it?"

"I know," Liza commiserated. "Its not like you can just snap your fingers and suddenly Rachel and Felicia are best friends again and sending each other jelly beans or anything."

Suddenly, a big smile formed across my face. "No, it wouldn't be that easy," I told Liza excitedly. "But almost!"

"It's jelly bean time!" Addie shouted as we burst into a math classroom on Friday afternoon with big cartons of beautifully wrapped jelly beans in our arms.

I could see everyone in the class suddenly sit up straight as we walked into the room. The kids were all staring at us, hoping there were some jelly beans for them in the boxes we were carrying. Just as I had in the first three classrooms we'd already visited, I felt awful for those few people who weren't going to receive any gift bags. But there was nothing I could do about it. I just had to stand there and smile sympathetically at the people who were hurt.

Addie walked right over to Dana's desk and handed her seven bags of jelly beans. Dana sat there grinning behind the mountain of red, green, and yellow beans, knowing for sure that she'd received the most in that class.

But plenty of other kids had gotten jelly beans as well, including Felicia. I walked over and handed her four bags of jelly beans. She read Josh's card first. Then she read the one from Carolyn and Sam, and the one from Liza and me. She smiled up at me, and mouthed the words, "Thank you." But the fourth bag obviously surprised her. Her eyes opened wide. For a moment, she looked kind of puzzled.

Next, Addie and I entered Mrs. Johnson's science class. Once again, Addie burst through the door, shouting, "It's jelly bean time!" But she wasn't as enthusiastic as she'd been before. That was probably because there weren't any Pops in this class.

But I had two friends in this class. First I gave Sam a bag of jelly beans from Liza and me, and then another from Josh, Felicia, and Carolyn. Then I walked over to Rachel's desk. I handed her four bags of jelly beans, and watched her expression as she opened the cards. She smiled slightly as she read the card from Marc and Marilyn. She winked at me as she opened the card from Liza and me, and then laughed out loud at what Chloe had written on her card. But when it came to that fourth bag of beans, her expression changed. At first she scowled, but then she took a deep breath, read the message, and gave me a questioning look.

I shrugged and moved on to the next person. "Here you go, Heather," I said to a blonde girl sitting behind Rachel. "Two bags of beans for you."

At the end of the school day, Liza met me at our lockers. "So, how'd it go?" she asked me.

I shrugged. "Okay. I'm just glad that it's over. I've spent far too much time with Addie today."

"Do you think our plan worked?" Liza wondered.

"I sure hope so," I said. "Because I've got no other ideas."

"Me neither," Liza sighed.

At just that moment, I saw Chloe and Sam walking down the hallway toward us. That was a good sign. Chloe was on Team Rachel and Sam was on Team Felicia. If they were walking side by side, then at least two of our friends had come to their senses.

Or not.

"Liza, Jenny!" Sam shouted out. "Thanks so much for the jelly babies! They're delicious. Do you want to pop over to my house after school today? My mum made some yummy scones with raisins!"

"Hey, I was just about to invite them over," Chloe yelled at her.

"You snooze, you lose," Sam said. She turned back to Liza and me. "Whaddaya say, mates?"

"Forget them," Chloe told Liza and me. "We just got the *Happy Feet* DVD. You know you love it when those penguins start to boogie!" She did a little tap dance. Then she stopped and scowled at Sam. "By the way, it's jelly *beans*, not jelly babies. When are you going to learn to speak English?"

"You have to be kidding me," Sam replied in her strong British accent.

Before Chloe could reply, Marilyn and Carolyn came over to my locker. They were both red in the face and hopping mad.

"I can't believe you took my blue sweater," Marilyn shouted.

"You stole my black jeans," Carolyn argued back. "Besides, I look better in that sweater than you do."

I sighed. Considering the twins were identical, that sounded kind of ridiculous to me. Come to think of it, this was all really ridiculous. I glanced over at Liza. Obviously, our plan wasn't working at all. Our friends were still fighting. And it was still incredibly upsetting. At least to Liza and me. Addie and the other Pops seemed to really be enjoying the feud now that it wasn't upsetting Addie's fund-raising efforts anymore.

"The animals are very restless today," Claire joked, referring to my friends and me.

"*Animals* is the right word," Sabrina laughed. "Have you smelled them lately?"

"Must be a new cologne," Maya giggled. "*Eau de kitty litter.*"

I sighed heavily and rolled my eyes. Ordinarily that would have made me furious. But today I had bigger things to worry about than what the Pops were thinking or saying. I was coming to the sad, final realization that life as I had known it was over. Nothing was going to make my friends reunite.

Nothing, that is, except maybe some help from Felicia and Rachel. Talk about miracles! There they were, walking side by side, laughing and smiling. Behind them were Marc and Josh. They didn't look angry with each other, either. I held my breath. Was it possible they were all friends again?

"What are you guys shouting about?" Felicia asked. She glanced over at Addie and the Pops. "You've gotta stop all of this fighting. You're making the Pops too happy."

Marilyn and Carolyn stopped their shouting, and stared at her. "*We're* making the Pops too happy?" Carolyn demanded of Felicia.

"Like you didn't start this whole thing in the first place," Marilyn demanded of Rachel.

"Come on, Carolyn. Lay off her. It's been a week already," Rachel said. She looked at the twins, Sam, and Chloe. "How long are you all going to keep this up?"

"How long are *we* going to keep this up?" Sam asked. "What about you two? Frankly, I'm sick of the whole barney."

"The whole what?" Rachel asked her.

"Barney. Fight," Sam translated. "I'm tired of you two arguing."

"We're not mad at each other anymore," Felicia assured her.

"You're not?" Chloe asked.

Rachel shook her head. "Of course not. How long could we stay mad at each other? The season's over. On to next year!"

"Exactly. We're friends first, " Felicia said. She smiled at Rachel. "Just like you wrote in your note."

Rachel looked at her curiously. "Like *I* wrote? You mean like *you* wrote."

"What are you talking about?" Felicia asked her. "That was what you wrote on the jelly bean card. The one you sent me anonymously."

"I didn't send you any jelly beans . . ." Rachel began.

"Come on," Felicia told her. "You didn't have to sign the card for me to know it was from you."

"But I didn't," Rachel insisted. She paused for a moment. "So it wasn't you who sent me the anonymous jelly beans, either?"

Felicia shook her head. "Why would I do that after what you did?"

Liza and I looked nervously at each other. "Um . . . guys, come on," I said quickly. "It doesn't matter who sent who jelly beans. I mean, what's important is that you're friends now and . . ."

"*You* sent them!" Felicia said, pointing at me.

"Well, not just me," I replied sheepishly. "Liza did, too."

"But why?" Rachel asked. "You guys had already sent me jelly beans."

"Me, too," Felicia said. She stopped for a minute. "You wanted me to think those jelly beans were from Rachel. That's why you didn't sign the card."

I didn't say anything. What could I say? That's exactly what had happened. I'd just pulled a little secret admirer thing on Felicia and Rachel. Unlike the Pops, however, I had done it for a good reason.

"I should have known you wouldn't apologize," Rachel told Felicia.

"Why should I?" Felicia asked. "You were the one who . . ."

"Stop it!" Liza shouted.

We all looked over at her, surprised. Liza never yells. Ever. Until now, anyway.

"I've had it. This whole thing is ridiculous," she said, lowering her voice. "The game is over. Done. The whole team is to blame for not winning, and the whole team gets the credit for getting into the championship in the first place."

"That's right," I agreed. "Neither of you could have won or lost that game on your own. And it's ridiculous to keep fighting over it." I looked at them. "Weren't you happier a minute ago, when you were friends again?"

Felicia sighed. "I guess so," she murmured.

"Me, too," Rachel agreed.

"Okay, so be friends," I told them.

Felicia smiled . . . a little. Rachel smiled back . . . a little.

"And if they're not fighting anymore, there's no reason for you to fight," I told the twins, Chloe, and Sam.

"I guess," Chloe agreed.

"Mates?" Sam asked her, holding out her hand. Chloe nodded and shook on it.

"Sisters?" Marilyn asked, holding her hand out to Carolyn.

"Always," Carolyn agreed, shaking her twin's hand.

"And you two are okay?" Liza asked Marc and Josh.

"Yeah," Josh said.

"Totally," Marc agreed.

"Great! Let's go celebrate the end of the war!" I suggested happily.

"We can all hang out at my house this afternoon," Rachel suggested.

"How about my house?" Felicia said. "The yard's bigger."

"We have a new flatscreen," Rachel told her.

"But . . ." Felicia began.

"We can hang out at my house," Liza interrupted, avoiding another argument.

"That sounds awesome," Marc said.

"Yeah," Josh agreed.

I felt my shoulders relax for the first time that week. We'd made a conscious decision to just stop the fighting and become friends again. What a relief. Starting Monday, I'd be able to eat lunch at my regular table. And I wouldn't have to worry about who I spoke to on the phone, or who I sat next to on the bus. There were no more teams in my group of friends. Life was back to normal.

Well, as normal as life in middle school can be, anyway.

You Decide . . .
Or Not

What's your decision-making style — snap decision or flip-flop 'til you drop? Do you avoid choosing sides in an argument, or are you a snap judgment / follow your instincts kind of decision maker? It's up to you to decide, if you can. Just take this quiz.

1. **You're at your fave restaurant, but you can't decide between a burger and fries or the mac and cheese. What do you do?**

    A. Order whatever your friend is having.
    B. Ask the waiter to come back in a minute . . . then two minutes . . . then three . . .
    C. Go for the burger. You had mac and cheese last week.

2. **Two guys are into you! It's a girl's dream come true. Or is it? Now you have to decide between them. What do you do?**

    A. Choose the boy all your friends think is the cutest.
    B. Go out with both of them a few times, and then decide which guy you're most compatible with. He's definitely the one!
    C. Decide not to decide, and become friends with both of them.

3. **Woohoo! Your parents have given you permission to decorate your room any way you want. That means . . .**

   A. Making a sketch, listing the materials you'll need, and heading to the home improvement store.

   B. Decorating your room to look a whole lot like your best friend's big sister's room. Most people think she's got really good taste.

   C. Months of looking at paint chips, studying magazines, and hoping you'll eventually figure out what you want.

4. **You're at the mall. There are two great outfits you love, but you've only got the cash for one. What do you do?**

   A. Poll your friends, then, majority rules.

   B. Try on both outfits, become more confused, and eventually walk out without purchasing anything.

   C. Purchase the outfit that will mix and match best with the other clothes in your wardrobe.

5. **Two of your pals invited you to the movies. Two other friends asked you to go swimming with them. You really want to swim. How do you decide?**

   A. Tell the girls who are off to the movies that you're going for a swim today. You'll see a movie with them another time.

   B. See if you can get your friends to go to a later movie so you can swim *and* go to the flick. That way everyone's happy, even if you're a little exhausted by the end of the day.

   C. Tell everyone you're sick and stay home so you don't have to decide what to do.

6. It's time to pick an after- school club to join for the year. There are so many to choose from. How do you decide?

A. You know that you love to spend afternoons in the museum sketching the paintings. Since that makes you happy, you join the art club.

B. You want to spend your after school hours with your BFF, so you talk it over with her. Eventually, the two of you decide on joining the soccer team. Soccer's not the first choice for either of you, but it's something you both sort-of like. A compromise works for you.

C. You notice that all the popular girls are going out for cheerleading. Since they always seem to be so happy, you decide to follow their lead.

7. Summer's coming. Your folks are being super-generous and offering you a choice. You can spend two weeks at a sleepaway camp, or go to the beach with them. How do you make this decision?

A. Try to get some friends to go to camp with you. If no one's up for it, you'll go to the beach with your parents.

B. Watch a lot of reality TV and see whether your favorite "characters" are more into surfing or hiking.

C. Go online and read up on cool camps. Then Google the beach your folks are visiting. Once you've got all the facts, you choose the place where you think you'll have the most fun.

8. **It's school election time! How do you decide who to cast your vote for?**

A. You listen to all the speeches, and then vote for the candidate you think can really make a difference.

B. You vote for the most popular girl in school, and then make sure to tell her you did — maybe she'll let you hang around with her.

C. You find out who your pals are voting for and then cast a vote for the same person. It makes sense. You and your friends usually have all the same opinions, anyway.

1.   A. 2 points   B. 3 points   C. 1 point
2.   A. 3 points   B. 1 point   C. 2 points
3.   A. 1 point   B. 2 points   C. 3 points
4.   A. 2 points   B. 3 points   C. 1 point
5.   A. 1 point   B. 2 points   C. 3 points
6.   A. 1 point   B. 2 points   C. 3 points
7.   A. 2 points   B. 3 points   C. 1 point
8.   A. 1 point   B. 3 points   C. 2 points

8-14 points: No question about it, you know how to make decisions. You are able to figure out what you want, and you know how to go about getting it! Rock on!

15-20 points: When it comes to making decisions, you can be easily swayed. Often you listen to what others are telling you to do. Remember, while it's okay to ask others for their opinions, be sure the final decision is one you make for yourself. After all, you're the one who has to live with what you decide.

21-24 points: Are you sure you want to read the rest of this paragraph? Maybe . . . or maybe not. You could read it later . . . or tomorrow . . . or . . . It's hard to tell what you'll decide to do in this or any situation. Your score shows that you run from decisions rather than try to make them. You've gotta face it — sooner or later, we all have to make decisions. And now's as good a time as any for you to start.

NANCY KRULIK HAS WRITTEN more than 150 books for children and young adults, including three *New York Times* bestsellers. She is the author of the popular Katie Kazoo Switcheroo series and is also well known as a biographer of Hollywood's hottest young stars. Her knowledge of the details of celebrities' lives has made her a desired guest on several entertainment shows on the E! network as well as on *Extra* and *Access Hollywood.* Nancy lives in Manhattan with her husband, composer Daniel Burwasser, their two children, Ian and Amanda, and a crazy cocker spaniel named Pepper.